THE CHALLENGE

Johnny Wade whirled on her like a wildcat.
"Get to your room with your mother," he said
harshly.

They went, but Nadine turned once. "Carl,
don't let them—" Her voice broke and they disappeared in the gloom above.

Then a curious thing happened. Johnny Wade
grew calm. Almost.

"Listen to me," he said. "Listen, you crumby
timber louse. I'll send you away to college. You'll
get out of town tomorrow and you won't come
back for two years. That summer you'll announce
your engagement, yours and—my daughter's. But
you'll go back again for two more years, and by
God, you'll learn to be a gentleman—as far as a
timber louse can, as far as the world can see!"

"Thanks," Carl Hansen said. "Thanks for the
offer. I'm sure Nadine wants no part of it and I
know damned well I don't. So to hell with your
offer and to hell with you!"

Johnny Wade moved around the table. "Have
you lived here since you were a sniveling brat
and never found out nobody crosses up John
Wade like this?"

"No," Hansen said. "And nobody will know it
in Illahute. Because I'm on my way tonight."
But at the door he turned. "I'll be back, though.
Someday. Nobody runs me out of Illahute and
makes it stick. Not even you. Because I belong
here, too. Remember that, Johnny Wade!"

Other Books by Nard Jones:

OREGON DETOUR
THE PETLANDS
WHEAT WOMEN
WEST, YOUNG MAN!
ALL SIX WERE LOVERS
THE CASE OF THE HANGING LADY
SWIFT FLOWS THE RIVER
SCARLET PETTICOAT
EVERGREEN LAND
STILL TO THE WEST
THE ISLAND

I'LL TAKE
WHAT'S MINE

by

Nard Jones

Cover painting by Saul Tepper

WILDSIDE PRESS

First Printing, April 1954

The ranger song "Mr. Rover Le Frapp," by Carsten Ahrens, is used by kind permission of the National Park Service, United States Department of the Interior.

I'LL TAKE
WHAT'S MINE

Chapter One

CARL HANSEN was the only passenger on the bus now. The others had debarked at Port Angeles or Port Townsend. And nobody in those towns had climbed aboard the scarred and weathered vehicle heading for Pysht or Neah Bay or—Hansen's destination—Illahute.

Except for the driver, Hansen was alone. He had taken advantage of that to make himself comfortable on the bench seat at the rear. He leaned lazily against the left-hand window and stretched his long legs on the leather. From that vantage point he could look out toward the Strait, beyond the bluff, at the angry white caps flecking the steel-gray waters. Or he could glance up through the rear window slanting overhead and see the heavy clouds, scudding much faster than the bus and in the opposite direction.

He was a tall man, sitting or standing, and he had tossed aside his hat because the crown kept brushing the slanted top of the bus. His short-cropped hair was the color of bleached hemp, and except for the crinkles around his eyes, Hansen's face was singularly unlined. A casual glance might tag him as twenty-five or -six; but those crinkles, and something about the eyes themselves, added something to the years. In any case, Hansen was not a man who would one day look older than he was.

His face was rather pale now, but something lay beneath the paleness that marked him as accustomed to the outdoors. It was in the set of his shoulders, in the ease with which he relaxed on the long leather seat, maybe in the thickness of the wrists. In some inexplicable way he did not quite fit the button-down soft collar of his shirt or the drape of his jacket. Yet obviously he had worn clothes like these for a time. The point his body and manner made, without seeming to want to make it, was that he had done without such civilized gear and could do so again, and at any moment.

Korea had done some of that, but the years before Korea had done even more. Most of it had been done to him around Illahute, where he was heading now again, in the rain forests of the farthest reach.

The bus was making slower work of it as they left Port Angeles behind, not only because the road was difficult, but because there were stiff head winds to buck. The gusts were coming out of the north and west, Carl Hansen noticed, down between Cape Flattery and the southern tip of Vancouver Island.

And because the rutted road was along the bluff of the seacoast, barren of all but twisted and gnomelike hemlocks, it was almost as if the bus were a vessel trying to make it out of the Strait of Juan de Fuca into the open Pacific. Like the squat-sterned purse seiner that Hansen could see out beyond the bluff. Carl had been on this bus or one very much like it when the illusion of a vessel was heightened by a wild north-coast rain slashing against the windshield.

But that seemed like a long time ago now. Just how long ago Hansen was hardly certain. Years no longer were an accurate gauge to the passage of time. Five hundred or a thousand years had come tumbling forward into the laps of bewildered humanity at Hiroshima. Or *was* it forward? Before Korea he had wondered about that. In Korea he ceased to wonder about it.

Like the native webfoot he was, Hansen found himself wishing it would rain. Then, gazing upward through the slanting rear window, he smiled at the wish. He wouldn't have to wait very long, the sky told him. It takes plenty of rain to add up to 120 inches a year. That was just the average around the half circle of the Olympic Peninsula, along Cape Flattery and south of there, where the town of Illahute lay. And in that deep timber at his jostling back, in the nearly impenetrable center of the Peninsula, 140 inches of rainfall was average.

There had been guys in Korea who wouldn't believe that, but Hansen hadn't tried to make them believe it. No more than he would have tried to make them believe in the size of the trees that can grow under such rains. He hadn't even opened his mouth when Bucky Peel said he'd seen the biggest trees that grow—the sequoias, the really big trees, the giant redwoods of California. What point in telling Bucky that somewhere in the deeps of the Peninsula there was supposed to be a great cedar twice as big as the biggest sequoia known to man?

No point at all—because Carl Hansen hadn't actually seen it. He had only believed in it since he was a kid in Illahute, and he knew that he believed in it still, and would go on believing in it until he found out for himself it wasn't there.

So he'd never mentioned the biggest tree of all. But he had figured this much: If a man had been to the Peninsula once, he ought to go back, God willing, just to see if it was real. Maybe there were other reasons, but in Korea he hadn't figured those too much.

Now he knew what they were.

He knew why he was heading back for Illahute. That was where his roots were, where he belonged, and in a sense he had been cut off and driven away. That he had to fix—and fix but good.

By the time he had got to Seattle and climbed a bus for the Peninsula he felt that his instinct had been right. And he realized, too, that he had been remembering all along that Nadine Wade was still in Illahute.

What's more, he remembered how, out in the corner of the dark Peninsula, when a timber beast comes off badly, he crawls into the woods a while to get himself together. After a time he comes out again, twice as dangerous and looking for a mate. If she happens to be a mate he thought he had or might have, once upon a time, that's all right too.

In fact, the saying was along the north-woods coast, it's good medicine for the timber beast. Because a second time his foes will have one hell of a time confusing him.

Thirty or forty years ago they used the term timber beast for an owner, one of the old kind who logged hell and high water and never cared whether trees grew again where he logged. But of late years, in Hansen's time, a timber beast had come to be any punk who couldn't make it in the woods.

Well, now they'd see.

The bus moved into the long curve that made its ragged arc just inside the rise of the Peninsula. Hardly realizing that he did so, Hansen hitched himself to the far window to look closer at the Strait, spilling at last into the Pacific, like the mouth of a great river. The bus had been traveling almost due west and now was turning south to meander along the coast toward Illahute. This was Cape Flattery itself, the farthest north and west a man could get in these United States, where the scattered hemlocks were dwarfed and twisted by centuries of fierce winds beating in from the northwest and southwest alternately and forever. Beyond the scattering of pygmy coastline trees the forbidding rockland tumbled precipitously toward the sea.

Was that the tree to which he'd brought Johnny Wade's big open car, skidding it to a reckless standstill in the spraying sand, and taken Nadine in his arms? For one swift moment he felt sure of it. Then the bus swerved away, bearing south.

Hansen settled back in the seat and lit a cigarette, ignoring the "No Smoking" sign. He supposed he was a damn fool, thinking he could pick out that tree from among all the others. Yet he'd be willing to bet on it, if there were a way to prove it, if it were a thing a man would bet on. How could he be likely to forget any part of what had happened that day?

He remembered how he had been walking by the hotel on a Sunday afternoon, a little the worse for wear because Saturday night had been a ring-tailed snorter. Johnny Wade hailed him from the porch of the hotel.

"Wonder if you'd do me a favor, Carl."

Johnny Wade, one of the town's two richest men.

"Or rather," Johnny said, "it's a favor for Nadine."

She'd been in high school at the same time as Carl, but he couldn't say he knew her, even in a high school as small as Illahute's. Hansen was only a part-time logger and still a punk, and wondering that Sunday afternoon what kind of favor he could ever do for the Wades.

It turned out that some girls had been visiting Nadine from Seattle, girls she planned to go to college with in the fall. Wade had been going to drive them as far as Port Angeles, where they could make better bus connections. But something had come up at the mill or in the woods, and he didn't trust Nadine's driving.

"I wonder if you'd mind driving them over to Port Angeles, Carl." Johnny Wade smiled down at him from the porch railing. He wasn't much like what you'd expect a lumber magnate to be; a small round man with mincing, almost effeminate ways and delicate tapering hands, like a woman's. But underneath there was something hard and authoritative that wasn't all money..

"Nadine will go along, of course. So you'll have company coming back," Wade said. "You can take my Packard."

That was what did it, the Packard. He wasn't immediately keen on the idea of driving a flock of girls anywhere. They might make fun of him, in the way that kind had, pretending not to, and so might some of his woods pals if they happened to catch him at it. Besides, he needed a shave, and if he did not smell of sweat, then certainly he must of last night's whisky. There had been a hell of an impromptu brawl in the Golden Slipper that Saturday night. He might even smell of that cologne Angie used.

Yet a chance to drive Johnny Wade's convertible touring job was too good to pass up. It never occurred to Hansen to wonder why Wade trusted him with Nadine, when it would be falling dusk before they could return together. He realized subconsciously that to Wade he was a logger, although of a special kind, perhaps, as he was the orphan of the man who had been, in a way, the town's preacher. A logger wouldn't be expected to make up to Johnny Wade's daughter; that occurred to neither Wade nor Hansen as the remotest of possibilities.

"O.K., Mr. Wade," he said at last. "Where's the car and when do I pick up the girls?"

"The car's around in back of the hotel and the keys are in the ignition lock. I think everybody's about ready now, if you are."

Hansen was taken by surprise. There'd be no chance to shave and change to a fresh flannel shirt. By the time he had driven the car around to the street, Nadine and her friends were there waiting.

The Wades owned the hotel, of course, just as they owned almost everything in Illahute that didn't belong to the Baker-Smiths. And Nadine's mother was a Baker-Smith, born in the huge gingerbread house between the forest and the town. But that place was open only in the summer months; the rest of the time, such Baker-Smiths as remained on earth lived in Seattle or California, where they had other houses.

Excepting for Mrs. Wade. Johnny Wade had fixed up a whole floor of the hotel for his own family, and, counting out occasional brief holiday trips, they lived there the year around. "I made my money in Illahute," he liked to say, "so it's good enough for my family and me to live in all the time." It was a thrust at the Baker-Smiths and a kind of punishment for his wife, who thereby had to suffer for the absentee ownership of her relatives. The town realized this, and Mrs. Wade never troubled to hide either her suffering or her contempt. Even back then, Carl Hansen understood that such begrudged popularity as John Wade enjoyed in Illahute was rooted in this public sadism of imprisoning his proud wife there year after year.

Nadine was tall and handsome, like her mother. But, unlike Sarah Wade and like Johnny, she was friendly. Thus while Carl's acquaintance with Nadine in high school had been slight, he had never been awed by her.

Now as the big convertible swung around he stared coolly and slowly at each of the girls in turn, hoping to embarrass them into some respect. He wanted no smirks and quick meaningful glances because they were going to be driven by one of Johnny Wade's timber beasts. Then, deliberately, he let his eyes stop at Nadine's high round breasts beneath her summer dress. He saw her smiling, friendly glance fade out and the color rise from her throat.

Instantly he was ashamed. He reminded himself that Nadine wasn't Angie Skykomish, and her friends were not the leatherbellies of the Golden Slipper. And to him Nadine seemed quite young, no more than a kid. He didn't know that the reason for this party had been Nadine's twenty-first birthday; and that made her a few months older than Hansen himself.

There were so many of them that there had to be three in the front seat, and the dark one with wicked eyes and a curious twisted smile crowded in beside him. Nadine introduced her, and then the others, with a kind of prissy formality, calling him "a friend of my father's." It made Carl feel good, and in a way he had never before experienced. Nadine had given him a new relationship in the eyes of the world; she had identified him as something else than Holveg Hansen's son.

But he was painfully conscious of Johnny Wade grinning down at them from the hotel porch. Hansen waved, trying to be casual, hoping to hide his nervousness, praying that the dark girl wouldn't smell the stale whisky and the shirt he'd worn too long.

Then he slid the big Packard into gear smoothly and waved at Johnny again, without looking back.

Things didn't go badly once they were under way. The girls hardly stopped jabbering all the distance to Port Angeles, but Hansen kept his attention grimly on handling Johnny Wade's car. Two or three times Nadine attempted to engage him in the chatter, then saw he preferred the sense of power and control that driving the Packard gave him. After that she let him alone, and in another mile or two it was as if they had all forgotten he was there. And that was how he liked it—on the way to Port Angeles.

Returning in the late afternoon with only Nadine was another matter. She again sat close, although now there was no necessity for it. And for a time she talked, and when she asked a question it was clear she wanted an answer. But it was several miles before he realized that this girl didn't have to ask direct questions to draw him out. He had admired how she had managed it, even when, at first, he resented it. The way Nadine managed it was almost like a trick she might have learned. It was a lot different from a conversation with Angeline Skykomish, the pretty breed, half Indian, half French. He supposed it came from being rich and associating with people who were rich.

"Papa says you know the Peninsula better than a lot of old-timers," she said as they returned to the edges of the rain forests.

"I guess I ought to," he told her. "I did plenty of tramping around in there when I was a kid. I didn't know enough to follow the trails—and there aren't many, anyhow."

"But didn't you ever get lost?"

"Plenty. But if you don't get panicky and keep going slow, you got to come to the edge someday. I found that out. Or you hit a creek or river and follow it down."

"I always heard that when people got lost in there they traveled in circles."

"I don't know as I ever did," Hansen said.

"But Papa says there are cougars and black bears, if you go back in far enough."

Carl nodded, grinning. "Sometimes you don't have to go in very far. But I always carried an old thirty-thirty. That made me feel safe. And if I ran out of grub—like I did twice I remember—I could use it to knock over a squirrel or catch a fish."

"A fish?"

Hansen laughed. "If you shoot into a quiet pool where it looks like a rainbow or a cutthroat might be, you stun him. If he's down there, he'll float to the surface, out cold, and you can pick him up with your hand."

Nadine was silent for a time, then finally she said, "You know, all this time I've lived in Illahute and never been really inside the Peninsula. I've never seen the Enchanted Valley they talk about. But of course you have, haven't you?"

"More than once."

"Is it as wonderful as they say? Are there cliffs three thousand feet high, and a thousand waterfalls?"

Hansen grinned at her eagerness. "I never did much counting or took any measurements. But it seems like the cliffs might be that high, all right, and it wouldn't surprise me if there were a thousand waterfalls."

"I suppose you've seen that giant tree, then? The one that's twice as big as the biggest redwood? Or is it just a myth, like Papa says?"

"I've never seen it," Carl Hansen told her. "But I'm

going to look for it again some time." He glanced upward at the spires of the forest's edge. "The great cedar. I don't see why it couldn't be. I bet if Johnny Wade had ever been as far inside the Peninsula as I have, he'd believe in it."

"But did you ever know anybody who really *did* see it?" Nadine asked.

"Woodpecker Hogan."

"Woody Hogan!" There was faint derision in Nadine's tone. "Isn't he an awful old liar?"

"Sometimes," Hansen admitted. "And sometimes not. On a thing like the big cedar he might be telling the truth."

"Papa says it's just an old Indian yarn." Nadine sighed, and the sigh moved Carl strangely. "All the same, I'd like to see the Enchanted Valley sometime, big tree or not."

"I'll be your guide, any time you say." He tried to sound careless and light, but he was afraid his voice shook a little.

"I was hoping you'd offer to take me," Nadine said, surprisingly.

"Now?" he asked, with deliberate slowness.

"Maybe not now. Not right this minute. But sometime."

"I didn't think you meant now. We'd have to get permission from your father." He laughed, feeling surer of himself. "Even if we did—which would be a time far off in a mighty cold day in August—there'd be plenty of talk in Illahute, wouldn't there?"

"I wouldn't worry about talk in Illahute, and as for Papa's permission—well, I'm sure he likes you, Carl, and I'm not a child."

"Neither are most folks in Illahute, but an O.K. from Johnny Wade is still a good idea on most things. It sure as hell would be on this one." Hansen laughed again, almost an uproarious cackle, like Woodpecker Hogan's laugh.

"I don't see what's so funny as all that," Nadine said.

"You don't? Why, you're not just a Wade. You're a Baker-Smith, too. The only two-toned Wade-Baker-Smith in captivity!"

"You're being very silly, Carl," Nadine said, and lapsed into silence.

Carl didn't try to pick up the conversation again, but the mere idea of guiding Nadine through the Enchanted Valley gripped and moved him more deeply than he would have admitted. He'd never before thought of the Enchanted Valley as a paradise. He hadn't thought of the Valley in any particular guise, because when you got that far into the rain forests of the Peninsula you had enough to see and watch out for, just being there and getting through. Yet if a man was in there alone with a girl like Nadine Wade, it could be paradise, all right, or something mighty close to it. Maybe as close as a man could expect to get on this earth, considering everything.

The clouds from the southwest were scudding faster across the sky; they were heavier and darker and had begun to sag low with unloosed rain. He stole a look at Nadine. Her face was lifted a little toward the sky and her hair was blowing back so that he could see her ear. It was a nice ear, perfectly formed, like all the rest of her, and seeing it gave Carl Hansen a curiously intimate feeling. Suddenly some of the things they had been saying took on new meanings, as if they had known each other a long time, and closely.

He followed her glance toward the lowering sky. "Maybe we better put up the top," he said.

"Let's don't. Not until we have to, anyway. If it's a soft rain, I don't mind at all."

For several miles now she had been sitting close, touching him. But he was experiencing more than that, something he had never experienced before, and which in his curious kind of innocence he did not connect with their proximity at all. It was as if electrical currents ran between them, in both directions at once. It became so marked that he mentioned it. "There's electricity in the air. Must be the storm coming up."

He would never forget Nadine's gentle laugh, almost a secret whisper. Until then she had been a girl, but now she was suddenly a woman with a woman's mysterious knowledge.

"I don't think it's the storm, Carl." She touched her hand lightly on his knee, and then he knew.

The rain began like a mist, but soon it came faster. Without a word, as if they had discussed it and agreed upon it, Carl swerved the convertible off the road, into the headlands of Flattery, and pulled back the brake near a gray gnarled hemlock larger than the other wind-blown trees. It was hardly a shield, and the rain was pelting now, but neither of them cared.

When he turned to Nadine her red mouth was open, her eyes staring at him wonderingly. With a knowledge as mysterious as her own, Carl recognized that she had not meant this to happen, but that, without really knowing why or how, she was going to let it happen. Her summer dress was one of those that buttoned from neck to hem with little cloth-covered buttons, and not all the buttons withstood his nervous, wild gesture, but Carl did not know that until later. He saw the rain beating against Nadine's throat and running in droplets like tears between her breasts. When he took her head between his hands to kiss her he felt rather than saw that her hair was already plastered against her cheeks with rain.

"The rain," he began. "We ought to . . ." But his voice grew too thick to finish whatever it was he had meant to say.

"You can keep the rain away from me, Carl."

Chapter Two

WHERE THE TIME WENT that drizzling Sunday evening Carl Hansen would never be sure.

Johnny Wade had expected them to be late, to get home after dark. Johnny Wade was no fool and knew how long it would take to drive that road against the rain gusts driving in from the Pacific. They couldn't possibly have made it before eleven, and the Wades knew that. Nadine knew it. Carl Hansen knew it.

But after two in the morning was something else again. And neither he nor Nadine had realized it was that late. He would always remember that Nadine wore a tiny wrist watch on a black ribbon, a high-school graduation present. Heavy in his pocket was a nickel three-dollar watch that kept good time—logger's time, anyhow.

But they hadn't consulted those timepieces. What difference had time meant that night? They'd be home eventually, and each would be up in the morning and no time lost.

"Just get me a sandwich and a bottle of Coke," Nadine had said when they stopped in front of the roadside dump for food. "I must look a sight. I won't go in."

He hadn't thought she looked a sight. She had seemed to him very beautiful, very desirable once again, there in the faint glow from the gaudy instruments on the panel of Johnny Wade's big Packard.

They had sat there eating the sandwiches and drinking the Cokes, the rain beating so hard on the convertible top that they had to raise their voices. The fellow who ran the dump had thought they were crazy, sitting out there in the storm. But it was too dangerous a night to monkey with a sandwich and a Coke and try to drive at the same time. Hansen might have tried it if the car had been a heap of his own, or if Nadine hadn't been with him. But with a sweet timber like this, and a car like this, and both of them belonging to Johnny Wade, he felt a little cautious. Strangely more cautious and protective than he had ever felt before in his life.

It hadn't been quite dark, certainly, when they left that gnarled hemlock near the Cape. The lightship, out by the Swiftsure bank, had begun to show its beacon, but there was still a pink-yellow strip of light above the

16

long Pacific horizon when the big car rumbled over the bridge that spanned the Soleduc and they bore west again for a straight-on glimpse of the lights on Destruction Island.

But of course, after that it was dark.

The rain seemed to beat ever faster against the canvas top and the windshield, so that sometimes the headlights meant nothing and he had to slow to ten or fifteen miles an hour. That was how they had gone past the little settlement of Ozette, hardly noticing there were few lights. That was how they had drifted through the old ghost towns where once big lumber mills had flourished, as big as any operated by the Wades and Baker-Smiths.

They had thought nothing of the fact that a light was blazing on the big front porch of the hotel, or that it seemed to be the only illumination in Illahute, searing through that curtain of rain.

"You hop out quick," Hansen had advised, "on the front porch, and I'll put the car around in back where it was. Can't figure out why your dad leaves a beautiful job like this out in the weather."

"What about me?" Nadine had laughed shakily. Then she was moving up the steps, and he was moving the big Packard around the corner of the hotel.

He could not remember afterward whether he had planned to rejoin Nadine for a moment on the rain-swept porch. He remembered only that he had decided to pocket the car keys and deliver them to Johnny Wade first thing in the morning. It was at that point that it occurred to him that it must be very late. He looked at his nickel three-dollar watch in the light of the instrument board, and whistled softly.

Still, he hadn't expected to find Johnny Wade on the porch when he came back to the board sidewalk by the hotel. He had half raised his hand and Johnny's name was just shaping inside his throat when Wade said, "Hansen!"

It was cold, like a blow with a wet rag. Hansen had heard Johnny Wade's voice cold before, out in the woods. But never like this, never quite like this. And it was an order, too. Hansen knew an order when he heard one. He trudged up the steps, trying to smile, beginning to feel like a guilty kid, holding the car keys out to him.

"I guess you thought we must've had an accident," Hansen said. He remembered that his voice wasn't quite right, that there was a sort of croak in it. But that wasn't because of what had happened out there near the tip of Flattery. It wasn't that his voice cracked from guilt, for no guilt was in his mind at that moment. The fear that was in him came somehow from Wade, there on the hotel porch—and it came from something beyond, through the doorway.

"Come inside," Johnny Wade said, and led the way into the big lobby. At first it seemed empty. Then by the dim light of the leaded-glass lamp on the heavy library table Hansen saw Nadine's mother, standing in the shadows, her lips a thin line.

Then he saw Nadine. She was crumpled in one of the big leather chairs, head down, sobbing. And he was shocked at how disheveled she really was. It was then that he saw, really, saw the places where little cloth-covered buttons had been and were no longer. A stocking was askew and torn. Her hair was a tangled mass, and Hansen was startled to see that her lips seemed bruised.

Standing there irresolute in the half-dark lobby, he had a strange, almost objective feeling that he had no part of this and was looking in at Nadine and himself and these two terribly grim older people. He thought: Crazy damned kids! Why hadn't they got her straightened around at that roadside dump? Or why didn't they think in the first place—just think, and keep driving for Illahute?

"It's after two," Johnny Wade said, all his false effeminacy gone. Then he waited.

Nadine raised her head. "Carl. Carl, don't let them—"

"Be quiet, Nadine," her mother said in a voice like icy steel. "Your father and I will handle this."

Swift anger flooded Carl Hansen then. He started toward Nadine, but Johnny Wade stepped in front of him. Johnny Wade was stocky and would have fought. But he was no longer young, and Hansen knew he would have won.

But he didn't want to tangle with Johnny Wade. "Can't —can't we let her leave, and then you say what's on your mind?"

Nadine stood up shakily. "Carl, I—I haven't told them anything. It's none of their business. Don't let them—"

She stopped because Johnny Wade had whirled on her like a wildcat.

"Get to your room, with your mother!" he snarled.

"I'll stay, John," Mrs. Wade said. She was glaring at Hansen with all a Baker-Smith's fiery contempt for a woods punk.

"I said get upstairs with her!" Johnny Wade said.

When they had disappeared into the gloom above, Wade said, "This won't take long, Hansen."

"I guess not," Hansen had said, growing angrier, not sure what wouldn't take long, but ready for anything. Johnny Wade looked as if he might spring.

But then a curious thing happened. Wade grew almost calm. He seemed to be trying to smile. But his voice was tight and he could not keep out the hatred.

"What has happened," he said, and stopped. "Has happened," he finished, with great effort.

"Why don't you leave it up to Nadine what happened?" Hansen said. "I'll face any music, but first—"

"*First!*" Johnny Wade gritted it through his teeth. It had no meaning. It was a word snatched from Hansen's mouth and spat back at him through Johnny Wade's teeth. "Look here, you crumby timber louse, you're listening to John Wade!"

Hansen felt himself grow tense all over, but he held. It took doing, but he held.

"I'll send you away to college. You'll get out tomorrow and I'll tell you where to go and who to see when you get there. You won't come back for two years, and that summer you can see Nadine again. We can announce an engagement then. But you'll go back for two more years, and by God, you'll learn. Above all, you'll learn to be a gentleman—as far as a timber louse can—as far as the world can see."

This man is close to crazy, Carl Hansen thought. He's close. Too close. Something's happened that he never dreamed could happen. But is it all Nadine and me? That didn't seem possible.

"Do you get what I'm telling you, Hansen?" Johnny Wade asked.

Hansen nodded. "I get it. You pay for my college. You try to fix me up so it isn't too bad that I happen to be the guy to make an honest woman out of Nadine." He was amazed at his own swelling hatred; he knew that it was fast becoming deeper than the hatred of Johnny Wade and that gaunt, skinny wife of his upstairs. "Then I suppose when that's done, and we're married, you fix me up in the big outfit—is that it? You make me woods boss of Wade and Baker-Smith, maybe even secretary-treasurer. Maybe even a vice-president. Is that the deal?"

He had not thought that Johnny Wade's face could become more crimson, the eyes more dead and cold. "You took quick advantage, didn't you, Hansen? You knew when your chance came . . ."

Wade's voice weakened and petered out. He put a fist on the heavy table to steady himself, then straightened again, looking at Hansen.

The words came with effort. "Nadine's . . . husband . . . will do all right."

Hansen stared at him. "What about Nadine in all this? How do you know—"

"That part is finished, isn't it?" Johnny Wade almost yelled. "Her mother and I will handle that part of it now, you can be sure. I'm telling you now what's up for you, Hansen."

How long he stood there, silent, Carl Hansen would never quite know. But he knew he would not be in Illahute in the morning. There was no chance now.

"I—I'm sorry about this, Johnny. Nadine's a good kid."

"You fool, you idiotic timber beast!" The deceptively small fist pounded at the table.

"I said Nadine was a good kid," went on Hansen evenly. "But you can take your offer and shove it. I'm sure Nadine wants no part of it right now, and I know damned well I don't!"

Wade moved around the table. "Have you lived here since you were a sniveling brat and never found out that nobody crosses up John Wade like this?"

"No," Hansen said. "And nobody will know it in Illahute. Because I'm on my way tonight."

He turned, feeling sick, dizzy, almost as if he'd tangled physically with Johnny Wade. But at the door something made him turn and say, "I'll be back, though. Someday. Nobody runs me out of Illahute and makes it stick, Johnny. Not even you. Because I belong here, too."

What had made him say that? At the moment, he hadn't believed it much.

He had just gone out of the hotel, into the rain, and up along the road over which he and Nadine had just driven so grandly in Johnny Wade's fancy convertible. He had walked through the night and rain, and got to Ozette at ten o'clock of a Monday morning. A ten o'clock almost as dark as the hour before sunrise, he remembered.

In the little hotel he had been sick, near pneumonia, for four days.

Then it was the Army and Korea. They had been waiting anyhow.

Chapter Three

As on that other Sunday he was remembering, it began to pour from the low dark clouds hovering above the bus to Illahute. Hansen had known that he would not need to wait long for his wish for rain, and now it had come. He kept his face close to the window as if to soak it up through the glass.

Because the bus was traveling south now instead of west, the rain gusts were striking it broadside. Occasionally a blast would literally lift the old bus from its springs, tilting it, making the driver grasp the wheel tighter. It was as if the wind let them know it could, at any time it chose, lift the whole man-made thing, wheels and engine and all, and flip it on its side as helpless as an overturned beetle in the road.

The driver glanced into the rear-vision mirror. "I wouldn't get too close to them windows if I was you," he warned. "Fact is, a day like this I wouldn't even sit on the weather side of this goddamn hearse. Them windows wasn't made for this run. They can pop out like they was splattered with a twelve-gauge from a foot away."

Meekly Hansen shifted across the aisle, on the lee side. "I remember now myself."

There was a speculative silence up ahead. Then the driver said, "That sounded like you used to live around here."

"Yes. But I've been away for quite a while now."

"You know something? I thought you looked familiar. I don't forget a face if it rides with me more'n once. People think I don't see anything but the road and their tickets, but I do." There was a pause, an invitation Hansen didn't pick up. "Mind if I ask your name?"

"Hansen. Carl Hansen."

The face in the rear-vision mirror brightened. "Hell, sure! Carl Hansen. You went off to Korea, didn't you? Prison camp. You've just come through the Big Switch. Am I right?"

"Right," said Hansen tightly.

"Sure. I knew it. Your old man was the preacher, wasn't he?"

Carl stirred uncomfortably. He answered with a nod into the mirror.

"I remember him. Big tall guy." There was another pause. "Say, that was an awful thing, wasn't it, the way that storm took your shack? Your house, I mean. You were lucky to be away that night. In the woods, weren't you?"

"At Camp Two," Hansen said.

"I'll be damned," the driver said, wondering at the fates. "A guy never knows, does he?"

"It's not something I like to remember," Hansen said.

"Hell, sure," the other said. "You got to excuse me sometimes. I guess I get too damned interested in people and what happens to 'em. Maybe that's why I don't forget a face."

At last he sensed Hansen's reluctance to talk and fell silent. The rain grew steadier, the wind changed its angle. Instead of sweeping across the surface of the Pacific and driving broadside at the road and trees beyond, it had lifted higher. Hansen could see the excitement in the tops of the trees. That kind of wind was capricious; it could strike down, briefly, with hurricane force, then continue eastward with gentleness, fondling the treetops with no more anger than a zephyr shows.

"Well, here we are—the great metropolis of Illahute," the driver ventured finally.

The calling of the destination wasn't necessary. Hansen knew they were nearing Illahute, the only place in the world he could call home. He had been watching the road unfold in his hard-won silence. He did not look off to the right at the flat green rock on which the Hansen shack once stood, not securely enough. Someone— not Holveg Hansen, the last of its tenants—someone had built it upon a rock, but it had not stood. Carl didn't need to look to know what the flat rock looked like, or the angry sea just beyond. He remembered.

He found that he remembered the town, too, exactly. There was little change in Illahute. The wooden buildings, most of them protected with cedar siding, had grown more weathered, perhaps, a little grayer. But there were no bright new buildings, and no gaping holes where buildings should have been and were not. Maybe the people inside of them had changed, or were different people altogether. Maybe businesses had failed, as they sometimes did in Illahute; maybe the bank building now housed a dry-goods store, or maybe the shoe-repair shop was a candy store. Carl was prepared for that. But over all, Illahute looked the same, and that was important. How important he had not realized until now.

In one glance he saw the old resort hotel, on whose porch Johnny Wade had stood smiling on that other Sunday, and far down at the end of Main Street, half hidden in its lower curve, was the Golden Slipper. The gaudy sign was gone. Probably blown down by the wind, he thought. Hansen wondered idly whether Angie Skykomish would still be there, or any of the other girls. It seemed unlikely; except for Angie, they had been transient ladies indeed, and none too young for their calling. But Angeline had been young, and she had belonged to the Illahute country—more so even than any Wade or Baker-Smith. Angie's mother had been a Haida, and her father a big French-Canadian woodsman down from British Columbia. It was said that Angie took her mother's name because she never knew her father's.

Hansen felt he had outgrown the Golden Slipper, but in a corner of his mind he resolved to find out if Angeline was still there. Because nobody could better give him the present score of things in Illahute.

He stood up gingerly in the bus, cramped and stiff from the long ride. When he lifted down his new bag, the few items of clothing and gear shifted around inside loosely.

"Is the hotel still the place for a stranger in Illahute?" he asked, wanting to show there were no hard feelings for that crack about the Hansen shack.

The driver was obviously relieved. "It's still the only place." He grinned. "Only you're no stranger, Mr. Hansen."

Mr. Hansen. That sounded strange, and also pleasant. It fitted in with nebulous ideas in Carl's mind. Would he really be Mr. Hansen now in Illahute, and not just Carl Hansen, the part-time logger, the preacher's son—the orphan of a man who wasn't really a preacher at all, some said?

"Anyhow," the driver said, "the hotel is the bus stop, so you can fall right onto the front porch when I swing the door open."

Hansen laughed suddenly. He had seen that happen more than once.

"I see you remember," the driver said.

The decrepit vehicle swayed to the edge of Main Street, which was really only a short swollen stretch of the highway before it became a dead end. In the gray mist the gingerbread of the hotel porch loomed close. "Oh-oh!" The driver looked up at Hansen briefly as he braked the bus. "The dragon witch and her brother are out on their rockers, so be careful you don't get bit. It's a hell of a welcoming party for hotel customers, ain't it?"

Hansen peered through the rain-coated windshield, trying to see the pair. Only in this part of the world, he thought, would a man and a woman be rocking on a porch during a rainstorm. In his blurred view, the woman seemed old, almost emaciated; the man beside her was nearly as thin, but his eyes burned fiercely through the shadowed rain. With a shock he realized that these were Mrs. Wade, Nadine's mother, and her brother, Henry Baker-Smith.

The driver seemed to feel Hansen's shock. As though in explanation, he said, "Some ways the Baker-Smiths and Wades didn't come off so well in late years. Don't know exactly the trouble, because God knows the lumber business has been O.K. everywhere else. Some say they've got too sour-balled to treat the men right. Except for Johnny Wade's girl, that is. She runs the hotel now."

Hansen swallowed. "Yeah, I—I heard that." He hadn't. He wondered why his heart began pounding, as if this gray Sunday were no more than a week away from that other one when the rain had beaten down so hard. He managed a grin at the bus driver. "Well, thanks for the ride, Mac. See you around."

"Then you're going to stay a while?"

"That's the idea," Hansen said grimly.

The driver laughed, swinging open the door. "I could think of a lot of other places I'd pick to come back to. But of course it beats hell out of war."

Maybe, Hansen told himself, turning toward the hotel porch. There was the Korean peninsula, and there was this one, and the whole damned Pacific between. But something right now gave him the same feeling about this one that sometimes he'd had about the other.

He dropped down onto the wooden steps of the hotel and smiled at the pair on the porch. Neither smiled back, but he hadn't expected them to. Mrs. Wade spoke up first. "It *is* you. I had just mentioned to my brother, when the bus door opened, that the resemblance was striking." She turned to her brother as though Hansen had quietly vanished. "You were wrong, Henry. You said it must be someone who looked like him, that he'd not show up in Illahute again."

Hansen's glance went from the old woman to the cold eyes of Henry Baker-Smith. He saw no response except vague hatred. "Yes, wrong," Hansen said. "I'm back and glad to be back, too." He glanced toward the cavernous entrance of the hotel. "Suppose I can get a room here, at least for now?"

The old lady gasped, as if at unspeakable effrontery. But Henry Baker-Smith saw the point. "It's a public inn. Only other place is the old Golden Slipper. You recall that, of course, Hansen?"

"I'd rather give my business to the hotel, if it's all the same to you."

It was a calculated insult, born of swift resentment. But it was something more than that, something missed entirely by the two people on the dismal porch. Hansen had spoken in a jargon unknown to him when he lived in Illahute before. A man can learn a great deal in the Army besides war and patience. During the long and useless hours of Korea he had picked up considerable knowledge, reflected in the almost hypnotic and nostalgic patter of men from everywhere in the United States. Many of them, if they were old enough, had made their livings in ways strange to Hansen, but he had listened. Moreover, he had observed and considered a great many shades and degrees of morality and ethics and philosophy.

But to the two on the porch this was no more than a casual insult, from an inferior who had insulted them before. Johnny Wade's wife had been pale already, and now she turned white as a drift in the upper valleys. Henry's hands gripped the arms of the rocker until his knuckles showed bloodless and bony.

Instantly Hansen felt ashamed. He hadn't returned to Illahute to badger old men and aging women. His sudden smile was honest and contrite. "Look here," he said, "I guess I've made mistakes. But I belong here, too. I don't belong anywhere else, and I—I want to get along."

There were no answers in words; but there seemed to be a clear answer in those bitter faces. Hansen reddened, then shrugged and hurried into the big old-fashioned lobby. It was exactly as he remembered it. The stiff wooden chairs with the dark leather seats; the heavy oak reading table with its leaded-glass lamp casting a yellow glow on newspapers and well-worn magazines; the thin Indian rugs on the pine board floors; the big gaudy picture of Mount Rainier over the battered key rack.

The lack of change surprised Hansen even as he approved it. He would have suspected that Nadine might insist on brightening the place. Somehow it was pleasant to believe that perhaps she too liked it as he remembered it. Or maybe those two on the porch objected to change.

The man behind the desk Hansen did not recall. He seemed about Carl's age. His face was both dark and florid, with a battered nose and eyes somehow too small and unpleasantly bright. His jacket was conservative and possibly not of Illahute; beneath was a sport shirt open at the collar. In lieu of a necktie, black hairs curled upward toward a thickening throat. There was no tinge of obsequiousness ready to break through the rugged surface. His greeting was not even a nod; it was simply an awareness that a guest had moved toward the desk and asked for a room overlooking the ocean. Had he received some signal from the porch?

Still silent, he handed Carl a pen with which to register, then turned to the rack for a key. Hansen was curious to see if his name would draw some kind of reaction, but the clerk moved from behind the desk and waited by the stairway, jangling a key impatiently. He made no move toward Hansen's bag.

With a grim smile Hansen replaced the pen, picked up his bag, and walked to the stairs. "You folks have a way of making a stranger feel at home here," he said.

Not a flicker of expression crossed the man's face. "We do the best we can," he said, and led the way upstairs.

"Out where the handclasp is a little stronger," Hansen said, trudging after him. Still no comment. As they reached the second-floor landing Hansen said, "Does Miss Wade live in the hotel?"

The other turned slightly, still moving. "Miss Wade?" For a moment he seemed not to know the name. Then: "Yes. The Wades have all this floor—since the place was built."

The room on the next floor was pleasant enough, even

inviting. The furniture was worn and out of style, but there were bright clean curtains at the windows, and beyond were the gray glistening beach and the Pacific rollers. Carl Hansen had wondered all his life what a room here would be like, and there was no disappoint-ment even though he had by now seen better.

"Anything else now?" the man asked, standing by the door.

"Thanks, no." Hansen was readying some change in the palm of his hand.

"You don't need to do any tipping," the fellow said, almost with belligerence. "I got some ownership here."

In some faint way he could not analyze, Hansen didn't care for the way this information was put. He wondered in what way this character had an ownership in the place, and what his relationship to Nadine might be. With the same insistent impulse that had provoked him down on the porch, he asked again about her. "Is Miss Wade around much?"

"She's not around today, if that's what you mean."

"That's what I meant," Hansen said, not hiding his anger too well. "I thought I might say hello. We're—old friends."

"I see." There was an almost imperceptible pause. "Maybe you'll find it hard to find old friends in Illahute these days."

Hansen's eyes narrowed. He leaned deliberately against the foot of the bed, fished for a cigarette, and lit it. The burned match he flicked toward the tray on the bureau, missing widely. "Let's go into just what the hell you mean by that," he said slowly.

For a moment there was nothing. Then the fellow shrugged and there was the ghost of a smile, as if he would retreat just enough. "You know how it is, Mr. Hansen. A guy goes away for a while, even a little while, and when he comes back people have changed." He was studying Hansen harder now. "I mean they get different ideas about—well, about one thing and another." His glance became thoroughly professional, shifting around the room. "If that's all, I'd better be getting back to the desk."

Hansen did not answer. When the door had closed he stood looking at it a long time. The owner-clerk knew his name, though he hadn't looked at the registry card,

and Carl was sure he hadn't mentioned it. Even if the
pair on the porch had signaled that he was poison, they
couldn't have wigwagged his name. Hansen was positive
that he had never before laid eyes on Battered Nose. A
man could get that kind of nose in the woods. A logging
camp would be a likely place in which to get a beak like
that. Yet Hansen remembered clearly, he felt sure, every
face he'd logged with. And when you spend your first
twenty years or so in a town the size of Illahute, you
aren't likely to forget the faces of any of its citizens.

Hansen rubbed a hand across his face and went to one
of the two windows and raised the swelled wooden sash
with difficulty to look out through the slow rain. The
big Pacific breakers were rolling in, thundering; he could
feel the ground swell shaking the foundation timbers of
the old building.

The hotel sat in a sort of cove—as much of a cove as
could be found in this rugged stretch of Northwest coast
—and the beach swung in to his right in a long curve of
sand and jagged rock. Without wanting to, he saw the
big green rock that was flat on top, flat as a table, maybe
a thousand square feet. There the Hansen shack had
stood, until the wild night the storm swept it into the
sea.

And then, also without wanting to, he remembered his
father.

Holveg Hansen had been one of the traveling "profes-
sors" who came to the Pacific Northwest to lecture about
Egypt or Africa or other faraway places that doubtless
they had never seen. But by the time Holveg had drifted
into Illahute, beating his way along the Strait in fish-
ing boat and lumber dray and on foot, as far north and
west as a man could beat his way in these United States,
the calling of "professor" was no longer one at which a
man could make a living. Probably nobody would ever
know whether the thing Holveg Hansen did then was
out of the spirit or only a display of remarkable inge-
nuity. And probably there would be debate as to that
as long as Holveg was remembered in Illahute. He had
been in town two days, the butt of loggers' jokes and
even of cruelty, when he disappeared into the Peninsula.
Nobody expected to see him again. But when he reap-
peared, more than a month later, he claimed to have
penetrated into the depths of the rain forests. He claimed

even to have seen the great cedar and to have carved his initials on its giant trunk. But most significant of all, he claimed to have received there in the dark green jungle the call from God.

The preacher and his little family were given the abandoned shack on the flat green rock. On stormy nights the sea spray would pound it as if it were the deckhouse of a vessel.

The women of Illahute knew that the Reverend Hansen drank and that he treated his wife most sinfully. But most of them came to the saying that for his past sins God had given him an eternal struggle with the Devil, right within his own soul. Whatever else he was, they said at the end of the gossip, he was a man who wanted to be good and to do good.

Carl's mother, who would always be sweetly anonymous to him, very much as she had been in life, often tried to explain Holveg to the boy. But on this subject Carl could never quite bring himself to belief. On the day he came out of the woods to find that the shack had been swept into the sea, he was almost glad. If what his mother had said was true, then she and Holveg were at peace together until the end of time. If what she had said was only to console her son, then at least *she* had peace and Holveg was destroyed.

That was how it seemed to him then, and he was surprised to find now in his maturity that he felt very much the same way now. He took one deep, long breath and shut the window slowly. He had decided to see if he could find Angeline Skykomish.

In the half-dark bathroom down the hall he washed up, straightened his tie, and put his raincoat and hat back on. As he came downstairs he decided to keep his room key in his pocket and avoid another encounter with Battered Nose. But there was no one behind the desk and the lobby was still deserted. This time, however, he saw something he hadn't noticed before—a loudspeaker box on the wall, just above the bright oil painting of Mount Rainier.

On the porch, the elderly pair had gone, their rocking chairs still moving gently as if they had left them only seconds ago. Hansen glanced upward and saw another loud-speaker, near the roof of the porch. So that was how Battered Nose had known who he was.

There was, Carl decided, a simple explanation for most of the world's mysteries if you looked carefully enough. What delight Battered Nose must find in eavesdropping electronically, squatting behind his desk and listening to the jokes of traveling men and the whispered confidences of schoolteachers at vacation time!

Whistling softly, Hansen went down the wooden steps and into the rain. The smell of the sea and the dropping mists and the forests was good, mighty good. And in his ears now was the elemental music of nature: the sound of rain and surf and wind in the trees. He stopped whistling abruptly because no tune of man could improve on that.

Suddenly Hansen felt better and fitter than he had in years. He felt like a young bull elk at the end of an Olympic summer, coming down the mountainside, roaring in the mating season. Hands deep in raincoat pockets, his jaw lifted a little, Carl Hansen sauntered through the rain, down the scarred board sidewalk toward the Golden Slipper.

Chapter Four

THE TOWN was strangely deserted, and Hansen remembered again that this was Sunday. Somehow in this interim between the Army and the civilian world he had lost track of time, of the days of the week.

In the rain, the scarred board sidewalk seemed resilient. There were two frayed paths across the timbers, fibers shredded from the solid wood by the calks of loggers' boots. Other coast and woods towns had paved sidewalks by now, but not Illahute. Alongside the asphalt highway that here was the main street, the walks presented a curious anachronism.

Across the street a lone logger was navigating aimlessly through the driving mist. There was a three-day growth of beard on his face, his head was lowered like a bull's, and his lips moved. Hansen grinned, thinking how little change there had been, really.

There was one change: that logger's hat. It was no disreputable felt wreck, but a hard helmet, painted a brilliant red. And suddenly Hansen realized that this was the symbol of a very great change indeed. Mechanization had begun in the woods before Hansen left Illahute; and he knew that Korea, like any war, must have increased it.

Well, wars changed operations in the woods, but they couldn't change the forest giants or the jungle growth crawling forever in their damp shadows. And he felt that wars couldn't change a logger much, except maybe for that hard red hat. It was not within Carl's experience that machines did very much to soften men.

When Carl reached the Golden Slipper, at the end of the street, its door seemed swollen fast in the rain gusts, never to open again. Hansen didn't test it; already he had spun the old-fashioned bell clap three times and he knew he wouldn't ring again. He knew it was rather foolish to expect that Angie Skykomish would be there still.

But then the knob did turn before his eyes, the door did open, and most certainly Angeline Skykomish was in Illahute, and at the Golden Slipper, and herself at the door to welcome him.

"Carl! Carl Hansen!" She was a more mature Angie than he remembered; not quite so tall, somehow, or rather more fully blown. The Indian blood had taken ascendancy over the French, but both were still there in the olive face, the flashing eyes, the strong laughing mouth. She stretched out both hands to draw him inside, and there slipped her arms around his neck and kissed him.

"This is a little more like it." Hansen grinned, catching his breath. "Until right now, I can't say my welcome home has been exactly cozy."

Something like alarm flicked across Angie's dark eyes, then was gone. She laughed again. "Perhaps it would have been a little different if you had come to Angeline first." There was defiance of Illahute in her tone.

"The bus stops at the hotel," Hansen reminded her. "I came here the minute I got my gear stowed into a room."

Angie's dark eyebrows raised quizzically. "So? You are staying at Nadine Wade's place?"

"I haven't seen her," Hansen said. "And after all, I didn't notice any new hotels in the town."

"Perhaps not new ones," Angie said, and led him into the front room. Carl saw that the nude paintings were gone from the walls. The rugged furniture and the dingy rug showed the scars of the Golden Slipper's brighter nights, but now there was a patina of faded gentility over the room. It had changed as Angeline had changed; faint respectability had entered while Carl Hansen had been away. He realized that the absence of the Golden Slipper's sign was not an accident of the wind.

"Let me have that wet coat, and I will find something to warm your heart, maybe."

She was back in a moment with a tray on which were two heavy glasses, a bowl of ice, and a bottle of rye. Hansen faced her with an approving grin. "You seem to be the boss lady here now, Angie."

Her round chin lifted. "I am not a madam, if that's what you mean, Carl. I haven't taken Tubby's place. This place isn't like you remember. It's not called the Golden Slipper now, you know. It's just—well, I guess people call it Angie's rooming house."

"Good for you!" Hansen said. "I'll transfer my bag over here before night. There's something about the clerk at Wade's place that I don't like."

Angie didn't answer until she had handed him a drink

and prepared her own. "Here's to your return to Illahute, Carl." She paused. "And I wouldn't move in here."
Her glance was swift, half mischievous and half ashamed.
"They call it Angie's rooming house, and that's what it
is. A logger can come here to rest, if that's what he wants.
But usually I have a good-looking girl or two, and I don't
avoid old friends—if I liked them a lot. So you'd better
stay at Nadine's hotel, Carl. You've come back to start
over again, and that's the place for you."

Before he could answer, she was running on, quite
seriously: "But it isn't like the Golden Slipper, Carl. Of
course it couldn't be, even if that's what I wanted. We
couldn't keep up with the big houses in the other towns
around. Most of the loggers have cars, and of course more
and more have families, too. But I like it this way. I'm
twenty-six now, Carl, and not getting younger."

Angeline's feeble grasp on respectability amused Hansen, but he hid it behind a swallow of rye. It was very
good rye, not at all like the redeye once served at the
Golden Slipper.

"What happened to Tubby?" Hansen asked.

"She died one night in her sleep," Angie told him. "It
wasn't very long after you left. I bought the place from
the bank. They were glad to bail out, and I was the only
one of the girls who had the money. The others drifted
off, one by one, as they do."

"As they had to," Carl said. "*You* belong in Illahute,
Angie." He looked at her. "A minute ago you said I'd
come back to make a new start. I don't know how you
figured that, but I guess it's true."

Angeline's dark eyes flashed fire. "Of course it is. Only
not exactly a new start. It'll be the first you've had a
chance at. You didn't have a chance before, Carl. You
were a damned good logger, and a damned fine man all
around—but who thought about that?"

Hansen grinned. "Well, seems to me Johnny Wade
thought of it some."

"So I heard." Angie smiled. "But that doesn't count
now. Of course you know he's—gone?"

"Gone? You mean dead?"

Angie set down her tumbler. "I thought sure you'd
hear about it, Carl, because—well, because it reminded
people of your father. I mean . . ." She groped for words,
gave up, then plunged on: "One day he went into the

Peninsula to visit the Trembling Mountain camp—you remember, the biggest operation the Baker-Smith and Wade outfit has back there?"

Hansen nodded. He'd worked the Trembling Mountain show.

"Only he never got there," Angie Skykomish went on. "And he never came out. It's been nearly two years now, Carl."

It made no sense at all to Carl Hansen. Soft as he looked, as nearly effeminate as Johnny Wade appeared, Hansen knew that nobody in Illahute could take care of himself better in the rain forests. Not in a thousand years and if the world began turning the other way would Johnny Wade get lost in even the very center of the Olympic Peninsula. And Hansen found it hard to believe that Wade could be ambushed by an enemy, or that he could have an accident serious enough to kill him.

"I suppose," he said slowly, staring at Angie, "he could have got sick and—well, just died in there. But damn it, Wade wouldn't get far off a trail even if . . ." He stopped, still staring at Angie.

"That's just it," she said. "Nobody can figure it. They couldn't then and they haven't yet. For a long time people were sure he'd show up. Even after all the search parties—and let me tell you the Baker-Smiths and Johnny's wife and Nadine damn near had the whole Peninsula cut down—even then people thought he'd show up again. Somewhere. If not back here on the coast, then maybe over on Puget Sound. I know there was a hunt everywhere."

Hansen was smiling oddly, lost in thought. Presently he said, "I understand what you mean when you say it reminded folks of my father. I suppose there were jokes about it." He set the tumbler down on the tray beside hers. A faintly troubled expression spread over his face. "Do you think that—that anything about Nadine might have set Johnny off?"

Angie smiled wryly. "Forget it, Carl. That wasn't what drove Wade into the tall trees. There was something else. And after Johnny disappeared, things got even worse around here. There's almost nobody in the camps now, and there's been a lot of mean talk."

"That's strange. I'd give a lot to know why."

"I hope you can find out, Carl. Because somebody's got to do something about it."

Hansen laughed as though deriding the notion, but his lean face grew intent. "Maybe I could," he said. "I learned a lot by leaving Illahute. A lot I never knew before. I wonder if it's enough."

Angeline Skykomish moved toward him and touched his arm tenderly. "It's plenty, Carl. I know men. I saw it even before you went away, and I can see it now, stronger and clearer than ever."

He turned to face that curious, almost motherly smile of Angie's. "There's been talk that you were heading back, Carl," she said at last. "That you've hooked up with somebody in Tacoma to log for the pulp mill."

"That's right, I have. There's an old Army buddy of mine in Tacoma, and we're hoping we can do a little business. But my God, how fast talk travels around here!"

"It wasn't the kind of talk that meant much to me," Angie said. "I figured probably you came back most of all to show Nadine Wade what you're made of."

Hansen shook his head as much in surprise as in negation, like a fighter shaking off a glancing blow. "That's a crazy notion, Angie! Nadine and I have no business with each other. I know that. I guess that's why I turned her old man down that night."

Angie shook her head. "You can't be sure of that until you've seen her again," she answered slowly. Her dark eyes met his squarely. "Whatever scheme you've got for the woods, Carl, you want to be sure about the Nadine part. Don't get them mixed up."

"I haven't," he said. "I haven't got them mixed up at all."

But his mind went back to how and what he had remembered on the bus, when the bus made its swing southward for Illahute, out there at the ragged end of nowhere.

"You'll know when you see her again," Angie Skykomish said.

Chapter Five

To HIS SURPRISE, Carl Hansen found himself suddenly tired when he left the Golden Slipper.

It was, he knew, a weariness of nerves and spirit rather than of muscle. The long ride in the bus, the strain of meeting old Mrs. Wade and her brother, and the swift recollection of Holveg Hansen—all had combined to sap his energies.

Then too, there had been the curious enmity of Battered Nose, the hotel clerk who somehow seemed more than he pretended. Hansen had learned the secret of that enmity from Angie.

The man was Jake Murchison, and somehow he was the living symbol of all that had happened to the big outfit, to Mrs. Wade and her dried-up brother, even to Illahute and the Peninsula itself.

As he walked through the town, seemingly deserted in this Sunday downpour, he realized that it *had* changed, and in ways too subtle to be revealed by the weathering of its meager buildings, its houses along the fringe of the forests, or its shacks strung drunkenly above the sands of the beach.

He was glad when the old hotel loomed ahead in the dusk. He saw the rickety outside stairway against the rear of the building, each narrow landing marked by a door opening into the main hallway of its floor. Feeling his room key in his raincoat pocket, Hansen decided to enter by the back stairs. It was a short cut, and he had no desire to see Murchison again until morning. He had decided he needed sleep more than food.

The rear hall doors were left unlocked as a fire precaution. Not a light showed anywhere in the rear of the building. Obviously business was not rushing. And no lights were showing on the second floor, which Murchison said was still occupied by the Wade family. One of the dark windows was open and the edges of bright curtains floated out in the breeze. He stood uncertainly a moment on that second landing, staring at the open window. Was this Nadine's room? And was life now so bleak and dull in Illahute for her that she was already inside it and asleep?

Softly Hansen climbed to the next landing and let

himself into the hallway. The old floors groaned with every step as he made his way to his room and went inside. He was even more tired than he had realized. By now all thought of food had gone, and he had to force himself into a hot tub in the dingy bathroom once he had peeled off his soggy clothes.

The ancient brass bed had seen better days, and hard usage since. But Carl Hansen had found rest on harder pallets both in and out of Illahute.

He woke suddenly hours later and instantly knew why.

He had wakened because, just as suddenly, the wind had died and the rain had stopped.

He lay staring at the open window, hungry now, listening to the surf. He wondered if he should get up and try to find something to eat, or whether to roll over and forget it. Finding even coffee and a sandwich would be, he remembered, a problem in Illahute at that hour of a Sunday night. Or was it already the early hours of Monday morning?

He decided to forget it. He raised himself slightly to turn over, and found himself trembling with premonition, transfixed in that half crouch.

It seemed to grow lighter outside, very quickly in an odd yellowish way; and then he saw a ball of fire at his window. It dropped inside and rolled toward the bed, illuminating the whole room as he sprang naked from the covers.

Hansen's first wild impulse was to crouch against the floor, away from the explosion that a thousand rushing memories out of childhood and Korea told him came next.

But it was not a fragment of meteor. It was not a strange ball of fire following an electrical storm. And it was not a grenade, or a tongue of hell out of a flamethrower. With the smell of kerosene and burning rags in his nostrils, Hansen smothered it with his still damp raincoat. But that was not quite enough. Little devils of red-yellow flames danced out from under the coat in a staggering line across the dry and dusty carpet. Hansen grabbed for the blankets of the bed.

When he was sure he had killed the flames, he leaped to the window and peered out. There had been plenty of time for the thrower of the burning brand to flee. The shadows beneath the old hotel were empty, and so was the beach beyond. Turning again to the room, trembling now with rage, Carl carefully pulled blankets and rain-coat away from the smoldering mess. The stench of kerosene and rags was chokingly plain. The brand had been a ball of greasy waste, tied carefully together with what loggers call haywire.

Unthinking in his anger, Hansen wadded blankets, coat, and smoldering mass together and heaved them from the window, as far out as he could toward the beach. He jerked open his suitcase, rummaged angrily among its meager contents, and pulled on a pair of slacks and a heavy turtle-neck sweater. In another moment he was racing downstairs in bare feet.

The lobby was deserted, oddly quiet as he stood there. The only light came from the ancient reading lamp on the library table. He heard a clock ticking somewhere beneath the shadowy painting of Mount Rainier. He padded softly toward the desk and saw the clock near the lower tier of the key rack. It was a few minutes before two.

Hansen leaned far over the desk and made sure that no one was behind it. Then he raced for the veranda, vaulted the railing, and sprawled on the still wet boardwalk in front of the hotel. Had it not been for that fall, he might have raced around the old building without noticing that there were blazing lights behind the drawn shades of the second floor. It was nearly two in the morning, but someone was wide awake in the Wade layout on the second floor.

Hansen lost no time in getting up there. He rapped twice on the first door he came to, then turned the knob and pushed hard. It was unlocked. He almost fell headlong into the room. It was, he saw at once, the big long parlor that stretched clear across the front of the hotel, the parlor Hansen had heard about all his life and never seen until this moment. He was aware of the thick green carpet, and paintings on the walls, the heavy overstuffed furniture—but only dimly.

What he saw at once, and fully, was Nadine.

"You'll know when you see her again," Angie Skykomish had said.

He saw Murchison, too, standing near her, turned toward him now with an expression of sudden fear and hatred. And he saw old Sarah Wade, standing in the half shadow of a door that Carl guessed must lead to her room.

But what he saw fully was Nadine, staring at him with her frank blue gaze, half surprised now but without the fear that was in Murchison's eyes. What he saw was Nadine, tall and straight and proud, her breasts round and high beneath a smart dress he felt he remembered even while he knew he could not really remember it. For women had dressed a little differently when he left Illahute. And this was not entirely the girl Nadine whose friends Hansen had driven to Port Angeles in Johnny Wade's car, at Johnny Wade's imperious suggestion.

And yet it was, too. It was nearly the same girl that Carl Hansen, there in this room, at this strange hour of the morning, still filled with anger, and with that horrible smell of burning rags and kerosene a stinging madness in his eyes, remembered clearly.

He remembered too well; and even in an anger that seemed now a hatred flaming like that ball of fire, Hansen knew that Angie Skykomish had been right. Nadine was surely part of the reason he had come back. Maybe he'd find she was all of it.

Murchison's was the first voice in the room, guttural and snarling. "What the hell's the idea, Hansen? Busting in Miss Wade's apartment like a wild man, half dressed. Are you drunk?"

Hansen ignored the last half of the question. "You're damn right I'm half dressed. But I'm interested to find you three all ready for the great outdoors. Do you want to know why, Murchison? Or do you already have a pretty good idea?"

"Why, Carl?"

Angie Skykomish, wise as she was, had been only half right—or she hadn't told him all of it. He'd know when he saw Nadine again, Angie had said. But she hadn't warned him that he might know still more when he heard Nadine's voice, when he heard it saying his name in a soft question. It was like a blow, glancing against his cheek—like a blow a man welcomes, the start of trouble he has known must come.

He hoped he was keeping his voice even. "So you don't know, Nadine? Or you, Mrs. Wade?"

From the old lady in the doorway there was only a

faint contemptuous sound. Murchison stepped forward and Hansen braced to meet him. But Nadine's hand was on Murchison's arm quickly. "No, Jake. Wait!" She smiled at Hansen, in that quick way he remembered. "Mother and I just got in," she went on quietly. "We've been over to Uncle's for Sunday dinner. Jake just told us there was some kind of commotion in the hotel, and we thought we smelled smoke."

"You did," Hansen said shortly. "Maybe you were supposed to smell it from your uncle's. Maybe the rain held Mr. Murchison up a little." Carl was feeling a lot better now; the trembling was only inside him now, and somehow it was a different kind of trembling. "But when the rain stopped, I woke up. If that hadn't happened, you might have smelled something else. Have any of you ever smelled human flesh burning?"

"Nadine!" called the old lady querulously. "That fool is insane!"

"I'll take care of him, Mrs. Wade," Murchison said. But Hansen saw that he still stood there, Nadine's hand on his arm. "Look here, Hansen. You haven't any right to come busting in here insinuating a lot of things. If you've come back to Illahute to make trouble, we'll—"

"I didn't come back to make trouble. But it looks like I'm running into some, Murchison, and somehow I don't feel like running the other way. And I'm not insinuating, I'm just supposing. I'm supposing that maybe you've put a slug of insurance on this dump, and on top of that you don't much like the idea of my coming back to town."

For a moment Murchison's expression did not change. Then his lips and even the battered nose seemed to be trying to twist his face into a smile. "Why should I care whether you came back or stayed away the rest of your life, Hansen? One less half-baked whistlepunk when you left. One more now that you're back. Just one more half-baked whistlepunk looking for a job."

"Carl!"

Nadine's voice kept Hansen's bare feet where they were planted on the floor and pulled his punch waist-high. Nadine's voice saying his name almost in command. And a second later he was grateful. He had to talk to Jake Murchison about timber, and it would be tough enough to get a deal out of Murchison without stretching him on the green carpet now. If he'd hit near the mark about that ball of fire, maybe that would help some in a timber deal, too.

"I'm not looking for a job as whistlepunk or anything else," Hansen said slowly. "I've come back to Illahute to make a deal for some timber. Baker-Smith and Wade have got most of the timber out there." He looked at Nadine, then back to Murchison. "And I was told that nowadays when you want to make a deal with a Baker-Smith or Wade, you have to talk to a guy named Jake Murchison."

"Jake!" It was Sarah Wade again; she had moved into the room, her wan face even whiter now with anger. "Throw this upstart out of this room. Throw him and his baggage out of the hotel!"

Nadine turned. "Just a minute, Mother. I'm running the hotel. We won't throw Carl out." She swung around again to Murchison. "I've known Mr. Hansen a long time. Why don't you be a good boy, Jake, and let us have a visit?"

Hansen grinned. "You ought to investigate the smoke," he suggested.

Murchison's face contorted in a way that made Carl want to burst into triumphant laughter. "Look, Nadine," Murchison said. "You better take your mother's advice about Hansen . . . *this* time."

Hansen saw anger flicker across Nadine's blue eyes, then something a little like fear. Her face seemed to grow paler, but she stood her ground. "You heard what I said, Jake. If the fire was in Carl's room and he's put it out, why don't you go to bed?"

Hansen did not need to see Murchison's face to sense that only white-hot proud anger gave Nadine this courage now. He was sure she feared Jake Murchison in a way that went beyond physical fear. And the old lady had been against her, too—against them both. Yet she was sending Murchison away.

When Murchison left, old Sarah went too, slamming her bedroom door with all the contempt that a Baker-Smith could muster for a Carl Hansen out of the woods, a timber beast that had had the unspeakable audacity to take a daughter of a Wade and a Baker-Smith into his arms completely.

Chapter Six

HANSEN AND NADINE stared at each other for a long time when Murchison and Sarah Wade left them alone together.

Carl did not know how long it was before he was aware that she was smiling—that half-amused but friendly smile that he remembered.

He looked down at his bare feet in the lush green pile of Johnny Wade's carpet. He found himself taken back over the years and into the embarrassment of another Carl Hansen, a younger fellow he believed he had left far behind.

Suddenly he heard Nadine's bubbling laughter. "Oh, Carl! Carl, what a way to call on a girl after all this time!"

At first her laughter flicked him, and then he joined it. He joined it because he knew suddenly that Nadine was ready to laugh with him at the absurdity of this union of two people who had been, if only for a little time, very close. Whatever strange spell had been between them a moment ago was broken now, melted into something that was better and held more promise. Yet it was something that Carl Hansen could not define.

He tempered his laughter into a wry grin. "Maybe it isn't the way to call on you, Nadine. But my welcome to Illahute hasn't been exactly bright, either. When I stepped off the bus onto the hotel porch, your mother and uncle seemed to want to cut my throat. Not that I blame them."

"Carl, it isn't altogether because of—of that night. Uncle Henry and mother have been through a good deal since . . ." Her voice faltered, and Carl put in quickly:

"I know, Nadine. I heard about your father. I'm sorry."

"And you mustn't think that Jake—that any of us—had anything to do with what happened tonight."

He looked at her questioningly. "Any of *us?*" he repeated.

Her eyes wavered, and she half turned from him. Against the glow of the lamp he saw the sweet curve of her breast, and remembered. Against the glow of the lamp her corn-colored hair was like a halo. And he saw that she was tall and strong, completely a woman now—a woman for any man out of the woods.

Easy, Hansen, he told himself. This got you once, re-member. And she's a two-toned Wade and Baker-Smith; she's everything both families mean; everything that you seem to be against.

But the self-warning was no good. He found himself going to her, standing close, touching her. She looked up at him and something like fear filled the blue eyes. That isn't fear of me, Hansen thought. It's fear of Murchison.

He took her in his arms then, and felt the thing he had felt so long ago, that electrical current between them.

"Carl, no!"

He kissed her, softly at first, and then harder. Her arms were strong against him. Her head drew back, her eyes were wide and sober and filled with earnestness. "No, Carl. This isn't right. This isn't the way. Not yet."

He found himself dropping his arms and stepping back. She smiled. "Go back to your room and get some sleep, Carl. We—we can talk again tomorrow."

He went back to his room then, and lay on the rum-pled bed. But he did not sleep. It was strange how she had made him do that, he thought. It was almost as if she had led him there and put him to bed, almost as if he were a child.

You'd better stick with the likes of Angie Skykomish, he told himself, staring at the dark ceiling. Nadine Wade isn't for you. She's the thing you're against.

At last he thought he had fallen asleep, but it could not have been a very deep sleep, because he heard foot-steps in the hallway. They were a man's footsteps, and they were vaguely familiar. Sleepily he tried to remember where he had heard them—and then suddenly he knew. He remembered Murchison leading him up to this room.

They slowed almost imperceptibly in front of his door, then went on. Down the hall was the faint sound of a key in a lock, the opening and shutting of a door, and then the click of the key again.

Hansen sat up in bed, rubbing his face roughly. There had been something he had meant to do, something he had forgotten. Suddenly he knew what it was and leaped from the bed to draw on the trousers and sweater again. Softly he let himself out of the room and went down the hallway, downstairs into the quiet lobby, around the old hotel onto the beach.

But the half-burned ball of greasy waste, which he had

wrapped in blankets and his coat and flung from the open window, was gone.

The whole thing could have been the nightmare of a drunken logger, up from a bout with Angie Skykomish at the Golden Slipper, for all he could say now. He could say that Murchison—or somebody certainly—had tried to toast him to a crisp and burn the old hotel into the bargain, maybe for the insurance or just for the hell of it.

He could say that, and Murchison could laugh. The whole town could laugh their heads off. Old Holveg's son, a chip off the block, had come back to Illahute, and was in town less than five hours when he was seeing a ball of fire floating into his bedroom window! He had hurled it back again, at the sky!

But of course, before it happened, he had been down at the Golden Slipper, having a few with Angie.

He figured it would be best not to talk about it. It was with that resolve, and a vision of Nadine's face in the lamplight, that Carl Hansen found sleep at last.

But next day Hansen felt the need to talk to someone, and midmorning found him again at the Golden Slipper. There he found Angie Skykomish had indeed turned over a new leaf. She was up, fully dressed, wide-eyed, and preparing the equivalent of a logger's breakfast, to which she promptly invited him.

"Get some of that coffee under your belt and relax, Carl. You don't look as if you slept much last night."

Somehow you played it straight with Angie. He wouldn't mention the ball of flame, but he felt impelled to tell her something else. "I saw Nadine," he said slowly. "And I guess you were right. There were some things I didn't realize until I saw her again."

He thought that a shadow went swiftly across Angie's dark face, but she laughed. "Now *that's* out," she said, "and you can go right ahead with your plan." She studied him a moment. "That is, if you think you can keep the plan and Nadine separate."

"I can," Hansen told her. "But what money I've saved isn't enough for the equipment, and I can't raise more cash until I've got a timber lease."

Angie's eyes flashed a dare. "How much money you got, Carl?"

"Around eighteen hundred, saved up from Army pay and lucky dice. But I didn't come here to ask—"

"I want to put in four thousand," Angie said. "Carl, you've got to let me. Woody Hogan was saying only last week you'd be back, and then we could—"

"Hogan!" Hansen stared at her unbelievingly. "Are you saying Woody Hogan is still on deck?"

Angie glanced at the ceiling. "If upstairs is the deck, then Hogan's still on deck."

Hansen swung around with a roar and bounded for the stairs. Angie Skykomish was at his heels, pinning him to the balustrade on the upper landing. "Now look! I've told you this is a respectable rooming house. There'll be no roughhouse and no funny business." She was half laughing and half serious. "Anyhow, I was trying to save Woody for a surprise."

"Where is he?" Hansen demanded. "*I'll* surprise the old goat."

"He's in his room," said Angie primly. "Probably asleep. Now you behave yourself and I'll show you where it is."

She led him to the end of a long hallway he remembered well. At the last door she knocked but there was no answer. She tried the knob slowly and opened the door. Woodpecker Hogan was not there.

As Angie's mouth went into a thin line, Hansen almost burst out laughing. "Now you just wait here," Angie ordered grimly. "I'll find the old hellion myself."

Hardly able to contain himself, Hansen moved one of the two straight-backed chairs to face the doorway, and sat down with arms folded. After a moment there was a commotion far down the hall, the sound of running water in a tub. Then he heard Hogan, protesting violently in his high, cracked voice. "Damn it to goddamn hell, Angeline, a fellow can't even try to take a bath around here without you thinkin' he's up to something. I keep atellin' you I wouldn't have nothing to do with that pair of spindle-shanked tarts you got in here, but every time I ain't right under your eyes you think I'm up to something."

"I know you, Hogan," Carl heard Angie say. "Now you march right down to your room. There's a man there wanting to see you, so I know you've been up to something, all right."

"A man? In my room? Waiting for *me?*" There was a moment of silence. "Damn it to goddamn hell, Angie, I won't go in there! Why should I? How do I know what he wants me for? What's his name and where's he come from, anyhow?"

"March!" Angie ordered. "I'm going downstairs and lock the front and back doors and keep both keys, so you might as well get in there and face the music, whatever it plays. And I guess you won't jump out any windows in your underwear."

"Don't be too sure!"

There was more silence, then the tentative padding of bare feet on the thin hall carpet. The footfalls grew slower and paused outside the door. There was a long moment until the door moved slightly and a grizzled little face below a shining bald dome peered in. The eyes flew wide and blue as the door exploded open. Woodpecker Hogan stood galvanized in flaming red flannel from neck to ankles.

"Carl Hansen! You young son of a beaver-eyed buck!"

They collided in the middle of the room, pounding each other's back until Hansen, not the seemingly frail old man, begged for mercy. "Hey, take it easy!" he yelled, pulling away from Hogan's ecstatic embrace. "Remember I've been out of the woods and in the Army—a sissy outfit!" He sat back on the brass bed, breathless and laughing.

Woody rummaged in the bottom drawer of the dresser. Triumphantly he fished out a pint bottle and unscrewed the cap. "This calls for the best panther oil money can buy, Carl, my boy. This ain't exactly the best, but it'll do, maybe." Hogan helped himself first to a quick snort and handed the bottle to Hansen.

It wasn't very good liquor; in fact, it was pretty bad. But Carl didn't mind. To him it was almost as good as Angie's first-class rye, because it came from Woodpecker Hogan, and because old Hogan was still alive and very much kicking.

The agile little man dropped to the floor cross-legged, an old habit of his. "Blew in last night," he said. "Been up at Angeles and Townsend, lookin' for work. But they all heard of me, so I was outa luck. And Illahute's dead from its rear end both ways." He took another pull on the redeye. "Aaaahhh! Now Angie tells me you came back to town with a bug up your britches leg. What is it?"

"Well, when I was in Korea I met up with a guy named Hollister. Turned out he used to work at the pulp mill in Tacoma, and planned to go back there. When he found out I was from Illahute and knew logging, we got to thinking maybe we could work out something. He got out before I did. He's in what they call wood procurement at the mill, and I saw him in Tacoma on my way back."

"Keep goin', son. I'm way ahead of you."

Hansen grinned. "I know damned well you are. Because all I got for equipment is not quite two thousand bucks." He remembered Angie's offer. "Maybe I could raise it to four."

"Money don't count as much as timber," Hogan said. "What you got there?"

"The whole damned Peninsula, if I can get a lease on some of it."

"If!" snorted Woody Hogan.

"The government's been making some good leases in other parts of the country, and if the big outfit isn't doing so well, maybe I can—"

"You mean Wade and Baker-Smith?" yelled Hogan, as if those were nasty words. "Look, son, you got as much chance of a timber lease from them as a pregnant fox in a forest fire. Less, now that Johnny Wade's gone." Hogan's eyes narrowed. "Are you figurin' to get mixed up with that Wade girl again?"

The sudden question startled Hansen. So Woody, too, was worried about that? "Look, Hogan," said Carl a little shortly, "I'm no kid any more."

"I know. But that don't mean nothin'. Look at me. I'm no kid either, but all the same . . ."

Angeline Skykomish had walked into the room, and Hogan let his boast subside sheepishly. "What do you think of Carl's scheme, Woody?"

"He ain't got no scheme worth dynamitin' until he asks me in on it, and he hasn't done that yet."

Hansen winked over Hogan's shining head. "Sure you're not too old now, Woody?"

Hogan's bare feet literally left the floor. "Why, you double-plated donkey puncher, I could lick you for fun every cock-blamed morning afore the wheat cakes. And you better take me in, because I know how to get the timber."

Carl laughed. "O.K., Woody. It's Hansen and Hogan and"—he looked across the room at Angie—"Skykomish."

"No, Carl. Let me be the silent partner. This has got to be respectable, and everybody knows I run the Golden Slipper."

Hansen nodded. "All right, then. Hansen and Hogan it is. Now where's your timber, Woody?"

"We can lease that whole hillside at Hemlock Creek Ridge from the Forest Service," Hogan said with the air of a pirate flinging back the lid of a treasure chest. "What's more, we can lease it cheap. You know that timber, Carl. It's sound stuff."

Carl snorted in disappointment. "I know it too damned well. It's sound stuff and will be till it rots—because nobody can get in there to get it out without spending a million for access roads. No wonder you could get a cheap lease from the Forest Service." -

"Unbutton your ears, boy. Remember how Hemlock Creek comes right out to the coast and empties up north here about a mile?"

"Yeah," Hansen said. "I remember it empties about a quart an hour in the wettest season. You couldn't float a toothpick down that stream, much less a pulpwood log."

Hogan, still grinning toothlessly, reached into his hip pocket and drew out a crumpled, dirty letter and handed it to Hansen. The letter was from the Inter-World Tractor Company, in response to one written by Hogan.

"Read what it says right there," demanded Woody Hogan. "They can make two high-cab tractors that will whip logs down that creek bed like it was a paved road. They've done it afore, back in New England."

A slow, wide grin spread over Hansen's face as he read the typewritten letter. He handed it back to Hogan with a wink. "There's no hair to speak of on that head, but there's sure a brain inside."

Angie giggled, and Woody Hogan pounded the rickety table. "You can bet the best pair of calked boots you got on that, son! Why, hell, we can whip logs down that there creek bed to the ocean, raft 'em, and float 'em around Cape Flattery to Tacoma as easy as pie."

"Hogan," said Carl Hansen, reaching for his hand, "I'm sure glad I got you for a partner."

Angie Skykomish put her own hand on their grasped fists. "Don't forget, boys, I'm in this, too."

"You bet you are," Hansen said. "And what's more—"

He stopped at a sound like a low growl of thunder outside the Golden Slipper. Hansen and Angie and Woody Hogan stared at one another. The sound was unmistakable. It was the sound of people, angry people.

Angie turned. "I'll go see."

"Stay where you are," Hansen said, putting a hand on her arm.

Almost instantly there was a loud rapping at the door downstairs. With Hogan close behind him, Carl ran to the hallway below and flung open the door. The porch was crowded with a group of burly loggers. Below on the board sidewalk stood the wives of some of them.

A spokesman stepped forward, a man Hansen recognized as Buck Flack, who had always been a mean man in the woods and a troublemaker. "Howdy, Hansen," Flack said with a threatening, sickly grin. "You too, Hogan."

"What is this, a welcoming committee?" asked Hansen.

"Not exactly. We hear you're planning to do some logging for the pulp mill in Tacoma."

"News gets around fast in Illahute these days. But I'm not set yet, if it's jobs you're thinking of."

"We could use work O.K.," Flack said, "but we don't want any pulpwood logging in these parts. Things been bad enough with the Wade an' Baker-Smith outfit, so we don't want anybody comin' in with competition. Some of them pulp and paper-mill outfits send their own fancy crews around."

"Flack, this is my deal—mine and Hogan's, here. If it works out, we'll run it. Who sent you down here to see me? It wouldn't be some of the Wade and Baker-Smith outfit, would it?"

Flack looked guilty, but he denied the question. "We're on our own, ain't we, boys?" The others nodded.

A woman saw Angie Skykomish looking from the window and shouted, "If you're in on this, Angie, you might find your place burned down yet!"

Hansen looked at Flack. "Buck, Woody Hogan and I have made up our minds to do some logging. If we can get a timber lease from the Forest Service, nobody's going to stop us. There may be jobs for some of you men. But not for you, Flack."

Flack made a quick movement, but one of the men

grabbed his arm. "Take it easy, Buck. Give 'em a chance to think things over. This is just a warning."

"That's what it is, all right," Flack said.

The group turned and clomped down the porch steps, muttering. Hansen shut the door and turned to Hogan and Angie. "Looks like it's not going to be easy for Hansen and Hogan."

"You ain't backin' down, are you, boy?" asked Hogan.

Hansen walked to the wall telephone and cranked for the operator. Turning to Angie and Hogan, he said, "I'm calling the Forest Service right now about that Hemlock Creek piece. If it looks O.K., I'll phone Hollister at the pulp mill in Tacoma right now."

Chapter Seven

NEXT DAY Hansen and Hogan rode the bus to Tacoma to talk with Hollister at the pulp mill and to meet the Northwest regional forester, who was flying up from headquarters in Portland, Oregon.

Hansen's telephone call to the Forest Service in Washington, D.C., had sparked a number of things at once, apparently. A recent Forest Service inspection had indicated there were signs of the Japanese beetle on some of the government spruce in the Peninsula. And the Hemlock Creek stretch was particularly vulnerable because the timber was getting past its prime. In a few years it might get beyond the harvest stage if the beetle got a good start. If someone could get the timber out now, the Forest Service would give its fullest co-operation.

Hansen and Hogan returned from Tacoma with the Forest Service's contract and a heady feeling of accomplishment. But after spending several days investigating the Hemlock Creek area and ordering equipment, Carl Hansen had a sense of weary reaction.

Only then did he understand that he had been straining for this for a long, long time—that this was the beginning of reality for those half-formed dreams in the Red prison camp. He was half tired and the muscles of his legs ached as if from tenseness. For a day or two he kept away from Angie and Woody and read in his room or on the beach—books and trade magazines on the latest logging operations.

It was three nights after the trip to Tacoma that he met Nadine on the sands of the beach. There had been, miraculously, a stretch of several days without rain, and of nights so clear that moon and stars were visible.

At first, in the moonlight, he became aware of a sort of diaphanous glow ahead, an outline he could not quite make out. Then suddenly he knew it was Nadine, walking the beach in a filmy summer dress that caught and threw out the moonglow in a curious way. They were walking almost in a line with one another, she with her head down so that he had to catch her by the shoulders to keep from colliding with her. She gave a little gasp.

"Carl! For the love of God, how you scared me!"

He laughed. "I didn't mean to scare you, but we were

about to have a head-on collision." He paused, looking down at her with sudden seriousness. "You know the outcome when that happens with us, Nadine."

She did not answer, and he asked, "Where you heading?"

"I was just taking a walk. I often take a walk on the beach when the tide is out and the nights are clear."

"I'll remember that," Hansen said. "Only it looks like most of the time now I'll be up along Hemlock Creek."

She nodded, looking up at him. "So I heard."

"So have most folks in Illahute," he said. "And it looks like some of them don't like it. Would you be included?"

"Why would I be against you, Carl?"

Take it easy, Hansen told himself. This girl is mixed up with Murchison.

"Well, a two-toned Wade and Baker-Smith *couldn't* like to see anybody mixing around in the woods of the Peninsula."

She didn't answer at once. They had veered away from the rolling surf to the dry sand. Suddenly Nadine stopped. "Let's sit down and you tell me about the Hemlock Creek job."

For just one moment he hesitated, remembering Murchison. Then it occurred to him that in any case the plans of Hogan and Hansen would be known from Port Townsend to Olympia within a few days. There were no secrets for long on the dark and rainy Peninsula, no matter how vast and thinly populated it was, no matter how difficult the transportation between towns.

He took off his coat and spread it on the sand for Nadine to sit on. "Woody Hogan gets all the credit," he said, and described how they hoped to drag logs down the trickling creek bed and raft them at the mouth. "Then we'll float 'em by tug around the Cape into Puget Sound and put them in the boom at the pulp and paper mill in Tacoma."

"Why, that sounds like a wonderful idea!" the logger's daughter exclaimed. "Why didn't *we* ever think of that?"

"Your outfit didn't have to. It's got all the timber there is. We had to scratch to find ours, and without the high-cab tractors and that creek, we couldn't afford to get at it."

"There's just you and Woody and the Tacoma pulp mill in the deal?" she asked.

He tried not to hesitate. Had she heard about Angie's stake? He decided on the truth. "Angie Skykomish insisted on putting a little money into it."

"I see." There was no more than that, and she fell silent. After a moment she said, "Papa would have liked that, do you know it? And he would have liked the idea of skinning those logs down Hemlock Creek, too."

"Maybe he would be doing it, if—" Hansen stopped, embarrassed.

"If what?" Nadine asked, and then very quickly: "Carl, I keep feeling he's still alive in there somewhere."

"Could be," Hansen said, trying to keep the doubt from his voice. "Johnny could take care of himself in the woods. Could take care of himself with an enemy, too."

"He could with a certain kind of enemy," Nadine said slowly. "One who wanted to use fists or beat him in a business deal."

"What other kind is there?" asked Hansen.

"I—I don't know," she answered strangely.

This is queer, Hansen thought, trying to figure it out. He had an odd feeling that she was holding back, that somehow she referred to Jake Murchison.

"If Johnny Wade is still back inside, why would he stay away so long?"

Nadine shook her head. "I really don't know, Carl. It's just a feeling I have. It isn't good for me. I've tried to get rid of it, but I can't. Mother and Uncle Henry don't believe he's alive. They say I shouldn't keep thinking so."

Hansen touched her wrist. "Maybe it *is* a good belief, Nadine. Anyhow, he's alive for you. I wouldn't worry about what your mother and Uncle Henry say."

She looked up at him, eyes wide and grateful. Suddenly he felt that strange electrical current between them, the thing he would always remember from that day in Johnny Wade's convertible. To hell with Murchison, he thought. I want this woman, and here we are again.

In a swift rough movement he took her in his arms and kissed her. But she pushed back with surprising strength, glancing fearfully toward the hotel. "No, Carl . . . please. We— Perhaps sometime . . . but not now, please."

Hansen drew back with a kind of relief that surprised him. Everything that Nadine represented was against him, and he had the warning already that these forces against him would increase. Yet somehow he seemed to have been inextricably bound up with her since that long-ago Sunday inside Cape Flattery.

"Remember once," he said, "how I was going to take you into the Peninsula?"

Nadine nodded. "Yes. To the Enchanted Valley of a thousand waterfalls. And maybe to find the great cedar. I remember."

"It isn't too late for that trip, is it?" Carl asked, smiling.

"I'm afraid it is," she said. "It's still a nice dream, though."

"We'll do it," Hansen promised.

She touched his hand lightly and got to her feet. "I must go back now."

Hansen picked up his coat and together they walked slowly toward the old hotel. He found himself trembling with a desire he had to control.

Chapter Eight

FOR THE NEXT SEVERAL DAYS Hansen was busy with Hogan in the Hemlock Creek area, cruising timber against the day their equipment would arrive. On that day the Hansen and Hogan show would begin. They had packed in and set up a rude camp, and when it was done, both returned to Illahute dog-tired.

They reported in to Angie, had a few shots of her rye and a hefty meal, then Hansen went to the hotel to try a bed for a change.

When he came downstairs next morning Jake Murchison was standing in the center of the lobby instead of behind the desk. He didn't look any happier than usual. "Hansen, come into the office a minute. I want to have a talk with you."

Hansen didn't like the tone of command, but shrugged it off. "O.K., Murchison."

Murchison led the way into a small office at the end of the long dark oak desk. To Hansen's surprise, Henry Baker-Smith and Sarah Wade were waiting there.

Hansen grinned at Murchison. "You said a talk. This looks like a conference. Maybe I ought to get my partner, Hogan."

Baker-Smith glowered. "*And* Angeline Skykomish, perhaps, as well. But it's you we want to talk to, Hansen. Sit down and let's get it over with." He looked again at Murchison, who had taken his place behind the small office desk. Sarah Wade sat tight-lipped, but Hansen noticed that her eyes, too, were on Murchison. This guy is sure a lot more than a hotel clerk, Hansen thought. He's taken Johnny Wade's place. I wonder how it happened.

"Hansen, I understand you and Hogan are going ahead with some pulpwood logging back in the Peninsula."

"We are," Hansen said. "In spite of your walking committee headed by Buck Flack. We figure it's a free country, and our timber is a lease from the United States Forest Service."

"I don't know anything about Flack," Murchison said. "And I don't know much about this being a free country."

He wouldn't, Hansen thought grimly.

"But I'd suggest, Hansen, you give it up."

"Why?"

Murchison hesitated a moment. Then a sickly smile began on his heavy lips. "Because we don't like it much."

Hansen held down his rising anger. He turned to Sarah Wade and Baker-Smith. "I've been away, you know. When I left here this character hadn't bought into your outfit. I like to know who I'm talking to. Is he an officer of the company, or just your trigger man?"

Murchison scraped back his chair, and at the sound Hansen sprang up. The thin sharp voice of Baker-Smith cut in swiftly: "Sit down, Jake." The old man turned to Carl with cold eyes. "Sarah and I are old, as you perceive. Johnny's gone now. If we choose to have Jake speak for us, that's our business."

"What about Nadine? She's not old."

Sarah Wade's eyes snapped. "Keep Nadine out of this, Carl Hansen—except for something I will have to say when you men are finished with this business."

Hansen sat quietly, still working to keep his anger cooled. Finally, with an effort, he turned again to Murchison. "As I get it, Hogan and I are to call off the Forest Service deal, tell the pulp and paper mill we can't cut the mustard, and cancel our orders for equipment?"

Murchison shrugged. "There are easier ways. For instance, you could transfer the whole contract to us. Then everybody would be happy."

"Except maybe Hogan and me."

"We could pay what expenses you've been out, and say five hundred each for you and Hogan. Of course there'd be an additional consideration. You'd agree not to try any more operations on the Peninsula."

Hansen grinned coldly. "It sure sounds sweet. And all this just because you don't care for what we're up to. All this because somehow, over the years, you guys have got a notion you own the whole damned Olympic Peninsula, even when you haven't been doing so good. Even when a lot of men are out of work."

"Our reasons are none of your affair," Murchison said. "This is a business offer."

"What if I said to hell with it?"

Again Murchison shrugged. "That wouldn't be a very good idea. That much you can bet on."

Hansen stood up slowly. "I'll bet the other way. You can all three go to hell."

Murchison's face purpled, but he knew he had his answer. "You're going to be damned sorry, Hansen—you and Hogan both, and that squaw down at the Golden Slipper."

Carl had been about to leave, but now he whirled. "Murchison," he said slowly, "if you include Angie Skykomish in any of your monkey business, you're a dead man."

"I think," piped up Baker-Smith, "we've got a threat of murder here."

Now old Sarah Wade spoke up for the second time. "We've something more. Proof that he's in love with that —that woman." Her eyes snapped hatred at Hansen. "Which brings me to what I mentioned a moment ago, Carl Hansen. You've been talking to Nadine about showing her the inside of the Peninsula. She told me. We'll have no more scandal caused by you, Carl Hansen. You keep away from Nadine."

Carl's heart seemed to leap against his throat. So Nadine had mentioned it to the old lady!

"Nadine's of age," Hansen said slowly. "I think she wants to go in there because that's where her father was lost." As he said this he glanced quickly at Murchison. He was sure that a startled shadow flickered across the man's eyes.

The old lady shook her head angrily. "She wants to go because you spoke of it when—before you left Illahute last time. And it's dangerous to encourage that silly obsession of hers that John may still be alive."

"I'm not encouraging anything," Hansen answered. "But if Nadine wants to see the region where her father disappeared, and asks me to be the guide, I'll take her. I'll take anybody else she wants to bring along. That'll be up to her."

No one spoke for a long moment. Then suddenly a torrent of rain swept the window panes and beat against the cedar shakes of the hotel. For a second or two the room seemed to tremble, and then the drops came steadily and there was the old sighing of the wind in the forest, the roar of the Pacific surf.

Henry Baker-Smith got to his feet, trembling. "The Army made you cocky, Hansen. You've forgotten just who you are in Illahute."

Hansen shook his head. "No. You've got it wrong. I've

forgotten who *you* are. I know who I am. Johnny Wade told me before I left last time. I'm a timber louse and a few other things."

"That isn't quite what I mean, Hansen. You're the orphan son of a crack-brain preacher and a woman he brought with him." Looking at Hansen's eyes, the old man stopped suddenly.

"Yeah, I know that, too," Carl said after a moment. "All the same, I turned down an offer to marry Nadine, which included some kind of job it looks like Murchison got. Also I turned down a free four years of college from Johnny Wade. But I decided on another kind of college."

Murchison moved around the little desk and faced Hansen. "You won't be so cocky in another month or so, young friend."

"We'll see about that," Carl Hansen said, and left.

He walked out into the pelting rain and, as always, listened for the muted music of wind and ocean and the soft fall of raindrops. Somehow he felt better now that the issue was joined between the big outfit and Hansen and Hogan.

He had walked perhaps half a block, whistling softly, when he was stopped by a shout from the hotel. It came from Murchison, on the hotel porch. He was holding aloft Hansen's suitcase. Carl grinned to himself. So I'm booted out of Illahute's only inn! At least it will save me some room rent.

Then his grin vanished. Murchison had dropped the suitcase onto the steps. It burst open and Hansen's few belongings scattered in the muck and rain. With that gesture Murchison turned and started for the lobby.

He did not quite make it. Carl Hansen covered the distance to the hotel porch in exactly the same time it took Murchison to walk across it. He grabbed the heavier man by his coat collar, spun him around, and smashed a left against his jaw.

Murchison sprawled against the old doorframe, so hard that the whole front of the ancient structure seemed to shudder. He began sliding down, then caught himself, shaking his head, turning and pulling upright again.

Carl waited. Suddenly Murchison stiffened. He swung like a bolt of lightning. Hansen had not expected that speed from so stocky a specimen. He weaved, but not enough, and the blow struck against the side of his head like a sledge. His knees felt watery and Murchison blurred.

Inside Carl's head something warned, like the trigger of a gun, Rush him. Move at him . . . or you're dead. It came down out of the past, that warning, down out of the trees behind Illahute. Carl rushed in close.

It worked. His legs stiffened and his vision cleared, and he was pounding at a rim of flesh around Murchison's middle. He worked his right around to a kidney, but Murchison was quick to make him remember that he had kidneys too. They staggered, grunting, embraced like grotesque lovers, and went through the old railing of the porch as if it were paper.

As they struck the wet board sidewalk Hansen rolled swiftly away. He was on his knees while Murchison still lay prone. He was on his feet again when Murchison had pulled himself only half upright, like a mud-soaked bear.

Hansen waited a moment. Then he said, "The suitcase, Murchison. Pick up that gear and put it back in the suitcase."

Murchison looked at him, hate glowering out of the squinted eyes. But he walked to where the luggage had sprung open, and bent down as if to obey the order.

Hansen waited for what he knew would happen next. He knew now about that incredible speed. Murchison seemed to straighten, and rush, and swing his left, all in one motion. But Hansen's left cracked first. He furnished only half the power and movement of that one; he let Murchison furnish the other half. It struck like a pistol shot, and Murchison went down, this time on his hands and knees.

"The gear," Hansen said again. "In the suitcase. Really do it this time, while you can."

Murchison dragged himself upright, not looking at Hansen now. Without another word, and very quickly, so that nobody but Hansen would see it happening, he got the stuff back in the bag and snapped it shut.

Hansen dragged the suitcase from Murchison's hand. "Thanks, Mac. The service here improves all the time. I'll tell my friends."

He went on his way toward the Golden Slipper, again whistling softly—and a little painfully. His mouth was swelling. But he felt good, better than he had in a long time. Nadine had talked with Sarah Wade about the dream of the Enchanted Valley. And now the issue was joined between him and Jake Murchison, too.

Only one little thing bothered him about this last. He'd made Murchison eat mud without killing him. With a man like Jake Murchison, that could be bad.

But hell, that was how it was.

Chapter Nine

WITHIN THE NEXT TWO WEEKS the equipment for the Hansen and Hogan operation began arriving. With the two tractors they could start hauling lumber inside for the cook shack and crew's quarters.

It was a happy time for Carl Hansen, and possibly even a happier one for the old underdog Woody Hogan. Hansen was young and had a right to his dreams, but Hogan had begun his days as a hired hand in the woods and had expected to end them the same way. While his young friend Carl was overseas, the old man had dreamed occasionally that Hansen would return with gumption enough for a show of his own, and that through him he might taste final victory. But he had not had too much faith in the dreams, because an old man knows too well the fruits of disappointment.

But now it was actually happening. Of course, as yet they hadn't logged a stick of spruce or raked in a dollar. But they were on their way to something, and the enmity of the Wade and Baker-Smith crowd only lent more zest to the enterprise as far as Hogan was concerned.

That was also true of Carl Hansen. He was out to show the town, and especially the Wade and Baker-Smith outfit—and, above all, Jake Murchison. But despite the needling of Hogan, he would not admit he was out to show Nadine.

When Hansen and Hogan were at the Illahute end of their operations they boarded with Angie Skykomish, who was always avid for information as to how the work progressed. Already she had made two rough trips into the Hemlock Creek region, and, overcome by the responsibility of partnership in a legitimate enterprise, had sent her two "girls" packing. The Golden Slipper was now completely respectable, and, as a consequence, its income was considerably reduced.

Hogan and Carl had remonstrated in vain against this move of Angie's. "Take it easy now," Hansen warned. "Hogan and I aren't dead sure yet what we've got back there. So far it looks good, but—"

"I don't care," Angie said. "Enough is enough, and I've had more than enough of the old life. I'm getting old and—"

"Old!" hooted Woody Hogan. "Look at her, an' she says she's getting old!"

Carl looked. Angie's smooth brown skin flushed slightly, and her dark eyes sparkled with French and Indian pride in her ripe beauty. She may have felt her years, but she was conscious, in the proud way of her Haidi blood, that she was handsome.

It was too bad, Hansen thought to himself, that probably she'd grow to be really an old woman in Illahute and no man would marry her because of her local reputation. And yet, he thought, why not? Angeline Skykomish, in her way, was essentially good. She was far better, Hansen conjectured, than many a "good" woman.

Then Hansen shrugged. Why need a guy get hooked up with anybody? At least right now. There was plenty to do. . . .

Hansen and Hogan and a small crew strapped up the first log raft at the mouth of Hemlock Creek a month later, and watched the little Diesel tug bear north for Cape Flattery.

They stood on a little knoll' on the north side of the creek and waggled their hard red hats at the outward-bound cargo. And the skipper of the log tug, sensing the occasion, waved back.

Carl and Woody were coming down the slope of the knoll when Hansen became aware of a slight figure climbing toward them. At first he thought it was a tourist hiker off the guide trails. Then suddenly his heart whirred like a frightened pheasant.

It was Nadine.

She wore hiking trousers and light trail boots. Over her blonde head was a snap-brim red hat, the kind hunters wear. Her shirt was a blaze of woodsman's colors, open deep at the throat. The strap of a light pack pulled the shirt slightly awry and Hansen glimpsed the cleft of her round breasts.

"Godamighty, it's that damned woman!" breathed Hogan in awe. "I got a mind to take a swing at her!"

"Shut up, Woody," Hansen said with a grin. "Maybe we got a chance to make peace with the big outfit."

"Peace!" spat out Hogan. "I know what kind you mean." He stalked off down the knoll toward the crew and the tractors, ignoring Nadine.

Nadine waved at Carl and came on up the slope a little breathlessly. As she got closer he saw that her face was quite serious. "Well," he said, "come to give our first raft a send-off? You almost missed it."

She arrived at his side. If she was beautiful in feminine things, she was even more impressive in this outfit, and an old thought came back to Carl Hansen. Here was a woman tall and strong, as well as courageous and beautiful; here was a woman for a man of the woods. Here, surely, was the mate for a timber beast.

Then Hogan's warning flashed in his mind, like a conscience, and he added, "Or did you come as a spy for the big outfit?"

Her hand flashed out and there was an explosion against his cheek. Then she burst into tears. When he tried to take her in his arms she pushed him back fiercely. The tears were gone as quickly as they had come. "I —I'm sorry, Carl. But I was all wound up. I've had a wild row with mother."

"A row?"

She nodded. "With the whole bunch, as a matter of fact."

Carl glanced warily down into the gulley, where he saw Hogan and the crew staring up at them. "How did it happen?"

She hesitated a moment. Then: "It's true I was coming up here to see your raft, but not to spy. After all, you told me about it, and I'm a logger's daughter. So when the word was going around town, I decided to go and see."

"I'm proud you did," Hansen said. "You're the only visitor we have."

"Mother saw me dressing for the hike and was furious when I told her where I was going. She phoned Uncle Henry and he phoned Jake." She stopped a moment, that old fear coming into her eyes. "Then Jake tried to stop me. That was just too much, and—and so I came."

She looked up at him, her eyes a little wild, and added, "So here I am."

"So here you are," Hansen said, "and you don't want to go back just yet. Isn't that right?"

"The way I feel now, I don't want to go back ever. But I—I don't know what to do."

There was a roar down in the gulley. One of the high-cab tractors was moving like a beetle along the wet rocks of the creek bed, heading back for the big timber.

"The outfit's about to start back," Hansen said. "Would you like to see the Hemlock Creek show?"

"Why, I— How long would it take, Carl?"

"The outfit won't make it downcreek again until tomorrow, maybe next day." He glanced at the light pack behind her shoulders. "Looks to me as if you could stand it overnight, and we can get more blankets from the bunkhouse. Are you game? Or will your mother and Murchison send out a search party?"

Her blue eyes flamed defiance. He had seen that blue fire before. "I don't care if they do. But . . ." She looked up at him seriously. "This could mean more trouble for you, Carl."

He took her arm and started down the slope. "I'll take a chance on that. Come on."

The crew had gone ahead in the lead tractor, whose throaty growls were growing fainter back in the woods. Hogan sat on the seat of the second tractor, one leg dangling, his weathered face a study in disgust.

"I believe you know Mr. Hogan," Carl said with a smile.

Nadine held a hand toward the angrily embarrassed Hogan. "I'm sure I know Mr. Hogan by sight, at least."

Hogan cringed, his face going beet red. "Same here, but I'm afraid my paw's too greasy to shake hands on it." He glared at Hansen. "You about ready, son? Or do you want we should be piloting this buggy after dark with no lights?"

"We're ready." Hansen grinned, giving Nadine a lift onto the cab floor.

"W-w-we?" gasped Hogan. "Is she goin' into the Hemlock Creek show?"

"Why, certainly," said Hansen calmly. "Miss Wade is very much interested in logging, naturally. Let her have the seat, Woody, and you and I will snake this buggy standing up."

If looks were weapons, Hogan's would have murdered Carl then and there. He slid out of the seat, muttering.

As the Diesel roared and Woody engaged the clutch with a jerk, Nadine held tight to the stanchions and laughed. All her fear and tension were gone now. This was adventure, this was something new—not dark and

foreboding, like the decaying old hotel on the beach—
and she loved it.

Hansen caught Hogan glaring at him in wordless
but bitter accusation. Suddenly he realized that he was
indeed embarking on something from which there might
be no turning back. And this could, as Nadine herself
had warned, cause more trouble from the big outfit and
Murchison.

At these thoughts he experienced a sense of guilt and
betrayal—betrayal of both Hogan and Angie Skykomish,
and perhaps himself. For a moment he fought with an
impulse to stop the tractor and send Nadine Wade packing back to Illahute.

Then he looked at her again and changed his mind.

The high-cab tractor lumbered along, its Diesel roar
resounding and ricocheting against the banks of the
gulley, against the great girths of the spruce and hemlock.
Under the control of Woody Hogan, who was none too
gentle with the handling, the tractor veered and yawed
over the round stones of the creek bed like a giant insect
feeling its way among obstacles.

There was little water in Hemlock Creek—a phenome-
non in such a rainy area, and due to some freak topog-
raphy in that part of the Peninsula. But sometimes there
were deep pools and Hogan avoided none of them. He
plunged the rugged vehicle straight through, making the
water spray outward from the treads. In some of the
deeper pools the water splashed over the engine hood
and against the windshield and flooded the floor of the
cab. Nadine laughed with the excitement of it and Carl
held her steady in the iron cat.

"Hey, Hogan, take it easy!" he called out once. "You
don't have to take all the rocks and ponds you see."

Hogan paid no direct attention to the plea. He glared
at Nadine with ferocious pride and said, "She works
mighty good, don't she, lady?" Then with a contemptuous glance at Hansen he added, "It was *my* idea, not this
lunkhead's."

On they roared, sometimes catching up with the lead
tractor and its own clinging woods crew. When that happened the two Diesels seemed to stir the needle leaves of
the forest giants like a wind, and it was as if the engine
growls were a continuous thunder.

The farther in they went, following the tortuous bed

of Hemlock Creek, the bigger grew the trees. They became thicker and taller, seeming to press against the dark sky. Occasionally the lumbering tractor pushed through a rain cloud that footed the earth. It was like moving through a dense fog, leaving their clothing and faces and hands as damp as from immersion in a lake.

Although Nadine had been born and raised in Illahute and knew the coastline of the Peninsula, she had never been this far inside, and she was awed.

"Wait," Carl Hansen said, almost yelling it above the Diesel's noise. "You haven't seen anything yet."

He didn't say anything more, and for several seconds was not exactly aware of what he had meant. Then suddenly he knew; and, moreover, he knew that Nadine realized his meaning as well.

When he had said, "Wait," he had meant the Enchanted Valley, the valley of a thousand waterfalls; and maybe he had meant something in which he believed but never had seen—the great cedar, the forest giant bigger than the biggest sequoia known.

"It's getting dark already!" Nadine exclaimed when the tractors had rumbled a mile or two farther on.

Hansen grinned and held up his rugged strap watch so she could see the dial. It was only a few minutes past three. Then he pointed upward beyond the roof of the cab. Far above in tiny patches the light of midafternoon filtered through. As they rumbled along, the sun came through the gray sky and suddenly a thousand shafts of light rayed down through the trees, spotlighting as many tiny pictures on the forest floor.

"Look here!" exclaimed Nadine, clutching at Carl's arm and pointing to a giant green fern sprouting from the underbrush and illuminated now by a shaft of light that seemed to come from miles above.

Hansen nodded. "It's a fine sight, all right. But wait. . . ."

Hogan squinted in the direction of the pale green brightness. "Horsetail fern," he said practically, and spat. "Millions of 'em in here." He glared at Nadine as if she might be the symbol of hated feminine nonsense about beauty and nature. "There's other things in here, too. Cobras and tigers and werewolves and fuzzy bats that drop down your shirt." He glanced significantly at Nadine's full bosom.

But Nadine joined Carl's laughter. "Woody," Hansen said, "I guess you named just about everything the Peninsula *doesn't* have in the way of animals and snakes and birds."

Hogan waggled his head wisely. "You two don't know everything that's in here."

They had grown accustomed to raising their voices against the concatenation of the tractor's Diesel. Voices shook with the vibrations of the powerful woods machine as it jerked over the uneven bed of the creek. "Tell me, Woody. Somebody—I think it was Carl here—told me you've seen the great cedar."

Hogan scratched his nose. "I'm one of the few who have—maybe the only one left livin' who has. They don't make the kind of men no more who can get to where it is."

"Papa always said it was a myth."

Woody Hogan snorted in derision. "Johnny Wade was smart, all right, but he didn't know everything. The big tree is real, don't you forget it. Carl's daddy was the only one outside of a real old-time woodsman to see it. He said he did, anyhow, an' I believe any old man of Carl's, even if he *was* a half-assed preacher. Excuse me."

It was tough to talk in the noise of the two tractors, and now they fell silent, lumbering through slowly increasing darkness as the forest thickened and the afternoon waned. In another twenty minutes the dim yellow lights of a cookhouse and bunk quarters gleamed out of small square windows cut into bright new lumber. The two structures stood in a fresh clearing, and beyond them were the high rig and other signs of the first cutting that had resulted in the raft now being towed toward Tacoma.

In the eyes of Nadine Wade, who had seen some of her father's logging shows near the coastline, the operation of Hansen and Hogan seemed a small one. But she was wise enough to understand that it could grow, and when she said she was impressed, she meant it. There was nothing small about the spruce and hemlock and Douglas fir that towered above the bright new shacks, dwarfing them and the equipment and the men and this one woman. There was nothing small about the great broad stumps, all that was left of the trees that had created the first Hansen and Hogan raft. Three or four men could stand shoulder to shoulder on almost any one of them. And the dusk air was heavily redolent of fir and spruce and the more acrid-smelling hemlock.

It was a smell that both Hansen and Nadine loved and responded to. As Woody cut the tractor's Diesel he saw Nadine take a deep, satisfied breath, saw the bright-colored woodsman's shirt tighten excitingly over her breasts. He jumped down from the cab and held up his arms for her. She sprang lightly to the soft, needle-carpeted floor of the forest. She looked up at Hansen, laughing. "I wonder if the search party is on the way yet."

"Can't tell. Woody and I haven't got radiophone communication. We'll get that later, when the operation is bigger."

Hurriedly, because of the falling darkness, he showed Nadine around. They were looking at a row of new power saws when the musical sound of the cook's triangle interrupted them.

"Hungry?" he asked.

"I could eat the proverbial timber wolf."

"Then the outfit of Hansen and Hogan invites you to supper. You are the first lady guest, I assure you."

Nadine arched her eyebrows. "You haven't had Angeline Skykomish?" she asked.

"No, not since the cookhouse was going."

Loggers consume great quantities of steaks, eggs, biscuits, and potatoes in a matter of minutes. On this night, surprised and embarrassed because of the presence of a woman, the crew finished supper in what doubtless was a record for the Peninsula. In less than twenty minutes Nadine and Carl had the long table to themselves. The cook had joined the men for a smoke outside and seemed in no rush to clear the table.

Hansen looked at Nadine over a thick mug of coffee. "I hope you forgive Woody for his manners. He doesn't care much for women, you know."

"Not for this one, I'm afraid." She sighed heavily. "I wish now I hadn't come here, Carl. It was a reckless thing to do. It's going to cause trouble between you and your partner, as well as make trouble for you outside."

Hansen laughed. "I'll handle Hogan. I'll handle the trouble outside, too. Do you think they'll send Murchison after you?" As he asked the question he watched for that shadow of quick fear in her eyes, and saw it come. Then her old defiance returned.

"They might," she said. "But of course I can't stay here after tonight, Carl."

"But you don't want to go back, do you?"

She shook her head. "No. At least not for now. I wish —" She stopped, and for a moment seemed helpless. "I was going to say I wished there were someplace else to go. But of course there is. I have friends in Tacoma and Seattle. I could take a long trip somewhere, I suppose."

"But somehow that really wouldn't get you away from Jake Murchison, would it?" He looked at her steadily. "What's his hold on you, Nadine? I'd like to know, even if it's none of my business."

"His hold isn't on me, Carl. Not on me alone, anyhow. It's on Mother and Uncle Henry. On the whole outfit. He drove Papa into the Peninsula. Mother doesn't know that and I can't tell her because it would kill her if she knew why."

"I don't get it," Hansen said. "I don't see how a man like that could do anything to Johnny Wade."

Nadine looked silently down at her plate for a moment before she spoke again. "You see," she said slowly, "Papa kept a woman in Port Townsend. I don't think anybody in Illahute knew that but me. She was Jake's sister. She died a little while after you left town, Carl, and that's when Jake showed up. He claimed Papa could have prevented her death, and threatened to tell the whole story if Papa didn't let him into the company."

"It doesn't sound like Johnny Wade to fall for blackmail. It's a wonder he didn't kill Murchison."

"I think he was afraid he might. I think that was one of the things that sent him away. But you can understand what it would do if Murchison told the story. Not just to Mother. The whole Baker-Smith family would turn against my father. And of course he never believed I knew anything about the—the woman."

I should have killed him when he threw that gear into the street, Hansen thought. It's a mistake to go halfway with a man like that. There won't be a better time than that was—but there'll be a time.

Carl spoke slowly. "Then he was the one who tried to burn me to a crisp, all right. He went after me right away because he figured I might be back in Illahute to take Johnny Wade's offer. The one I turned down the night I left."

Nadine stood up and walked to the window, staring into the black woodland night. He saw her pensive reflection in the glass. He went to where she stood. "And maybe that's why I am back," he said.

She shook her head. "No, Carl. You're back to make Hansen and Hogan the best logging outfit on the Peninsula."

There was a dry cackle from the doorway. "You can say that twice, lady. And if this sapling is smart, he won't try no mergers." Hogan glared at Hansen. "I built a lean-to for Miss Wade out under one of them blue spruces," he said. "Reckon that'll do her until she goes back tomorrow on the first tractor outa here."

Hansen lit a cigarette and spun the match at the big iron cookstove. "Woody, you can run this outfit for a few days by yourself, can't you?"

Hogan looked puzzled. But he snapped back, "There's no fooling about that, son."

Carl nodded. "Let's talk about it tonight before we turn in." Hansen's gaze turned toward Nadine. "You see, Hogan, Nadine doesn't want to go back to Illahute right away. And quite a while ago I promised to show her the Enchanted Valley—back inside."

Chapter Ten

AFTER Nadine had retired to the lean-to, Carl and Woody sat in the deserted cookhouse for more than an hour, mulling over the Hemlock Creek program for the time Hansen would be back inside the Peninsula.

Hansen did most of the talking now, unusual in any conversation with Woodpecker Hogan. But Carl sensed the reason for Hogan's guttural monosyllables. He was hurt more than angered at Carl's decision to guide Nadine Wade into the Enchanted Valley. Secretly, Hogan was eager for the chance to be top boss of an outfit in the woods, and Carl knew that. What Woody couldn't get straight in his mind was why Hansen was willing to cut loose at this particular time.

Carl knew that, too, and tried to avoid the question by sticking to business. "For the next week or so, keep sending Hollister big logs, like we're doing now, Woody. We'll make a showing, give him something to make pulp out of. But as soon as you're rolling, let's snake out some of the small stuff and the waste. Hollister doesn't object to that. It makes good pulp. And that way we save the big stuff for saw timber."

Hogan growled. "Dag-nab it, Carl, I hate monkeying with that little stuff. First thing I know you'll be wantin' to start up one of them cock-burned tree farms—and then's when I quit cold."

"That's *exactly* what I want to do." Carl laughed. "And you won't quit, either. You'll be the best damned tree farmer on the Peninsula!"

"I'll see myself in hell a foot deep before I quit loggin' trees and go to farmin' 'em," Hogan answered. "Maybe," he added, "that's something for you and the Wade woman to do when you get hitched."

"Who said anything about getting hitched?"

Hogan looked a little shocked. "Well, a woman like her don't go bargin' off back inside with a fellah like you, does she, unless they got in mind something serious?"

Hansen didn't smile. It dawned on Carl suddenly that while he was a tough old rooster who'd heard of everything he actually hadn't done or seen, nonetheless Hogan divided women into only two kinds: good and bad. Of course, Woody was not so naïve as to believe that no lady could own her secrets; but definitely he believed she should keep those secrets, and not involve others in them.

"I mean," Hogan went on, groping, "the whole danged Peninsula will know she's in the wilds with you. And that'll be double dynamite, because there's been talk about you and her before. Why would a dame like her take the chance?"

Hansen answered him quietly. "She's desperate, Hogan. The fact that she came back in here with us shows she's desperate. I'll be damned if I'm going to send her back there now."

"You could put her on a bus and send her to Tacoma or Seattle," Hogan reasoned. "Johnny Wade's daughter would have friends from hell to breakfast, wouldn't she?"

"Sure, Woody. And she's got them right here." Hansen swung around on the mess bench. "Look, you've got this wrong. Nadine's always wanted to see the Enchanted Valley. It's the truth that a long time ago I promised to guide her in there. Now she's got another reason. She kind of wants to see where they say Johnny disappeared."

Hogan was quiet a moment. "So you'll be just her guide?" he asked, not trying to keep the cynicism out of his voice. Carl nodded. "And," Hogan went on, "that's all you got in mind?"

Hansen's slow smile was on the grim side. "All that's any of your cockeyed business now, Hogan. Except this: If Nadine is set to drive a wedge into that Murchison-Baker-Smith outfit, I'm out to help." He looked at Hogan with narrowing eyes. "Maybe," he said slowly, "what I'm going to do will bring things to more of a head."

Woodpecker Hogan got up and tramped in a slow circle. He stopped, fixing Carl with a beady stare. "Now, that I can go for, son. But you might as well know I ain't too danged sure that's *all* that's in your mind. Maybe you should look into your submarine-conscience or whatever they call it."

Carl laughed, but he had the honesty to see that it was Hogan, and not himself, that gave a more realistic interpretation to his impending journey with Nadine. The truth was that he was anxious to get back inside—every bit as anxious as Nadine seemed to be. Their recklessness now seemed mutual. And he knew that it was mixed up with two vital concerns that had drawn them together once more. One was certainly that dream of long ago, their promise that one day they'd see the Enchanted Valley together. The other was a quiet but furious urge to break the dark bonds of Murchison. Hansen could feel that in Nadine; he knew the urge was strong in himself.

"O.K., Hogan," he said at last. "Let's just say there's more to this than meets the eye . . . *maybe*. And there can be some real trouble with Jake Murchison when he finds out Nadine is with me."

"You think you're givin' me news?" snapped Hogan.

"Be on the lookout. The grief could come direct from Murchison, or maybe through Flack and his mob, where the ultimatum came from."

Hogan cracked his first smile since Nadine had climbed aboard the tractor. "I wouldn't mind a hassle with Flack and his boys now we got strength of numbers. A damned good brawl improves production. Should we wait for 'em here, or go into town lookin' for it?"

"Wait for it here." Hansen laughed. "If there's any going into town for it, wait for me."

"You don't take a gander at the Enchanted Valley and get back in any four or five days," Hogan reminded him. From his sly tone he might as well have added: Especially when you go in with a looker like the Wade girl.

"Shouldn't be much longer than a week," Carl insisted. "We'll go downcreek with you first thing in the morning on the tractor, then drive in the roustabout as far as Hoh Ranger Station. I think I can borrow a pack horse there for part of the trip."

Hogan looked puzzled. "It's kind of a long shot to the Valley by that direction. How come you don't drive to the underside of the woods, and come in from the south?"

Hansen had to smile at how instantly suspicious Woody was about every aspect of this journey. "I hear Pete Baker is the ranger in charge at Hoh River. I was in high school with Pete, and I figure maybe he'll let us have the pack horse and let me take in a forty-five, at least, without a lot of red tape from headquarters."

Hogan shot an upward glance at the younger man. "Sounds like you've had the plannin' of this in your mind a long time. Well, go ahead. A logging boss that's off his trolley about a woman is about as much use around a camp as—as the *woman* would be." Hogan shot a meaningful glance in the direction of the lean-to he had built for Nadine.

Hansen sighed inwardly and gave up. There was nothing to be gained by trying to make this thing completely right with Woodpecker Hogan. It couldn't be done for now. "Well," he said, stretching his tall frame, "I guess we've gone over everything, Woody. What say we hit the sack?"

When they reached the bunkhouse it had long been echoing to the dubious symphony of healthy snores. Hogan was first to hit the blankets, and through half-closed eyes he watched the slower preparations of his partner. Several times Carl walked to the window and gazed out into the night where Nadine slept in the lean-to at the edge of the stumps. At last Hogan bolted stiffly upright in his bunk.

"I'll be the hind end of Babe the blue ox if ever I seen anything like the way that Wade girl has got you slippin' over the skid road!" he exclaimed heatedly. "It's danged near ten o'clock. Get stretched out!"

"Take it easy." Hansen grinned, turning. "I was just wondering if there ought to be a little fire near that lean-to."

Hogan squinted through the shadows thrown by the single kerosene lamp. "You mean you're scared she might get goose pimples in her sleep? That's all taken care of, son. I lent her your sleepin' bag."

"I wasn't thinking of the temperature," Carl said. "Don't forget we saw a cougar in here last week. It looked a little wild."

"That was last week," Hogan said, "before the crew started thrashin' around. But go ahead and build your little blaze. Then naturally, you'll have to sit there to watch it don't get out of control and start burnin' our slash ahead of time!"

Carl chuckled. "Hogan, I wish I'd got a partner who trusted me." He walked from the window, sat down on a bench, and began unlacing his boots. "I guess she'll be all right."

A new voice boomed out from a bunk near the ceiling: "Well, even if she *ain't* all right, she'll get more sleep out there!"

Hansen waved sheepishly. "O.K., Hank. Sorry."

But Woodpecker Hogan thumbed his nose in the direction of Hank's bunk. "My goodness, but you sleep delicate," he said in a squeaky falsetto. "I seen the time

when a redheaded logger could sleep through hell and
a boiler factory until the cook banged the triangle for
breakfast."

Hansen himself found it impossible to drift off to sleep
in his usual fashion, once he had stretched out on his
bunk. At what late hour he dozed off he did not know.
It seemed to him that he had not slept long when he
awakened again, and with the uncomfortable certainty
that someone had left the bunkhouse and now moved
quietly among the fresh stumps of the clearing.

He got up carefully and in woolen socks made a slow
round of the bunks. The only one empty was Woodpecker
Hogan's.

With mixed and puzzled feelings, Carl hurriedly
slipped into his boots and secured them with quick
hitches around the tops. A glance at the clock told him
that on the coast the first gray streaks of dawn would be
in the sky. But here on the middle reach of Hemlock
Creek it was still black as pitch as he slipped out through
the bunkhouse door. He moved toward the lean-to, skirting the big stumps almost by instinct until his eyes accustomed themselves to the darkness.

Three or four yards from the lean-to he nearly stumbled over Woodpecker Hogan. The scarred old codger
was dozing, back against a giant spruce, bony knees
hunched up, with a rusty hunting rifle cradled across his
lap.

Before Hansen could step back into the clearing,
Woody was on his feet. There was the cocking of the
rifle hammer, astonishingly loud in the crisp night blackness. "Hold it, Hogan!" Carl called in a husky whisper.

"So it's you," Woody answered, his cracked voice sharp
with disgust. "I mighta known it would be you." Plainly
he was embarrassed at Hansen's discovery of him there.
He tried to hide it with feigned anger. "Said to myself
it'll be young Mr. Hansen, Esquire, who'll be smellin'
around that lean-to, and no mad cougar. So I said to
myself also, I'm goin' to fool him. He can just hang on
to himself, I says to myself, until he gets on that picnic
into the Enchanted Valley. This here is a logging operation, I says to Woodpecker Hogan, and not a danged
boodwower."

Hansen held in his laughter with difficulty. But he
knew he'd better keep control over his amusement.

Woodpecker Hogan was caught red-handed showing a soft spot in his heart for a woman and was plenty upset about it.

"O.K., Woody. I'll get back to the bunkhouse." Hansen said it with simulated humility.

"Make it snappy." Hogan waved the rifle. "An' don't try to circle and come back or I'll wing you, so help me!"

As Hansen found his way back to the bunkhouse he chuckled softly. He knew that Hogan hadn't set himself on guard for the reason he stated. Hogan had got to thinking about that cougar, and about the fact that Hank, the redhead, and maybe some of the rest of the crew were curiously wakeful.

Yes, sir, Hansen thought as he settled down in his bunk, it began to look as if Nadine Wade was getting under Woodpecker Hogan's skin too. Such a thing had never been known to happen in all of Hogan's long life. But the more Carl Hansen thought about it, the less surprising it seemed to him. Nadine was that kind of woman. And the fact that she was ready to go gallivanting off into the rain forest with Carl Hansen, that she was ready to break away from the old and hateful roots in Illahute—those things, too, would weigh in the scale with Hogan.

Carl Hansen drifted into sleep smiling. He knew now that although Hogan fought against Nadine, he secretly admired her. And perhaps Hogan knew, with the wisdom of an old battler of the woods, that this was a fight he couldn't win anyhow. . . .

At the wash bench next morning Hogan growled to Carl out of the corner of his mouth, "Don't you crack your face in front of the crew or that girl that I was on guard duty last night!"

Hansen tossed cold soapy water out of the tin basin, mopped his tanned face swiftly with his towel, and winked at Woody. "I guess I just dreamed it, Hogan. I never let anybody know what I dream."

"I bet you don't," grunted Hogan.

Hansen glimpsed Nadine coming across the clearing. She waved and called a cheery good morning that included the whole crew. Carl watched admiringly, thinking she might almost be a part of the crew herself. There was no self-consciousness, no underlying impression that here was the daughter of Johnny Wade and Sarah Baker-Smith Wade. There was something about her easy carriage and her attitude among the men at breakfast that reminded Carl vaguely of someone else he knew. Suddenly, surprisingly, he realized that Nadine's natural and open honesty here was reminiscent of Angie Skykomish. He remembered the old line from Kipling and decided it must indeed be true that the Colonel's lady and Judy O'Grady are sisters under the skin.

When, as at supper the night before, the crew had its hurried fill and left them alone at the long board table, Carl said, "You haven't changed your mind about seeing the Enchanted Valley?"

Nadine smiled at him across the table. "As I remember, it was you who made my mind up. So the question is—have you?"

Hansen shook his head. "Last night after you turned in I went over everything with Hogan. He's going to take full charge for a week or so. We'll go downcreek this morning on one of the tractors and pick up the Ford roustabout. I figure to start from the Hoh River station. Remember Pete Baker?"

"Pete Baker? Oh, yes, of course. He was in high school with us, wasn't he? Sort of—well, fat, with lots of freckles, and very jolly."

Carl laughed. "I have a hunch he's worked off that excess poundage, because now he's the ranger in charge at Hoh. I don't know about the freckles, but let's hope he's still jolly, because I want him to help us outfit. Something tells me you don't want to go back to Illahute for anything."

"That's right, Carl. Mother would pounce on me and I'd never get away." Her blue gaze glanced off and Hansen knew that it was Murchison, more than Sarah Wade, that she feared. "I've got a light pack, you know. But not enough gear for a trip like that."

"It's enough for you to carry," Hansen said. "The going gets rough toward the White Glacier, and stays that way until we hit the Valley."

She looked at him dubiously. "I—I really don't want to try it if you don't think I can pull my weight. I'd hate to get back in there and fold up on you."

Hansen grinned, taking in the clear skin, the healthy blue sparkle of her eyes, the deep young bosom. He re-

membered the fierce jostling she had taken on the tractor the day before, and recalled her long, strong stride
in the clearing.

"You won't fold up," he said. "And maybe I can talk
Pete Baker into lending us a pack horse. We won't be
able to take the pack animal beyond the Hoh trail. After
that we'll travel light and make the best of it."

Nadine's eyes were shining like those of a child who
has been promised adventure. With a curious quietness
she said, "I'm so anxious to start, Carl. You can't imag-
ine what it means to—to get free of things for a while."

He nodded soberly. "I think I can, Nadine. But you
know, don't you, that it will be only for a while? A man
—or a woman—can't run away forever."

"I know that," she said, "and when I've come back,
when I've seen the Enchanted Valley and where my
father . . ."

She did not finish. Hansen cocked his head toward the
cookhouse doorway. One of the tractors was coughing
and growling into the day's activity. "It sounds as if we
can start, Nadine, if you're ready."

She drained the last of the strong black coffee in the
thick mug and stood up smiling. "I'm ready, Carl."

"Good! Bring your pack and the sleeping bag from
the lean-to while I pick up my stuff. I'll meet you at
the tractor in a minute or two."

At the bunkhouse he found his trail pack, checked it
for the essentials of personal gear. He tossed in extra
pairs of heavy woolen socks, a small first-aid kit, a sealed
pint of bourbon whisky. Gròping beneath the mattress
of his bunk, he found his .45 and a handful of shells.
He wrapped them all in a thin lightweight poncho and
added them to the pack. Then he checked the pockets of
his iron pants for the presence of his jackknife and the
waterproof tube of matches he carried from old habit.
In the strongbox of the Ford roustabout he knew he'd
find a runt machete and other equipment it would be
wise to bring along.

Woodpecker Hogan was ready too. A husky tow of
four great logs was already chained to the tail of the
high-cab tractor in the shallow creek. The big Diesel was
warming up in gentle powerful chugs while Hogan
slumped relaxed in the driver's seat, one skinny leg
swinging free. He had grunted a good morning to Na-

dine at the cookhouse, and now took little notice of either the girl or his partner. It was as if he were part of the tractor's equipment, simply ready to go into action at Hansen's touch. His only recognition of them was to slide off the driver's seat as Carl boosted Nadine into the cab.

"O.K., Woody. Let's go!"

Hogan braced his back against a stanchion. There was a mighty roar, echoing and re-echoing against the forest giants, rising with a banshee screech into the topmost branches that seemed to finger the opening sky. The jerking cleated treads peppered sizable round stones at the butts of the yawing logs that were chained astern. The heavy links of chain sprang taut, giving the illusion that at any instant they might snap like grocer's twine.

Then finally, with another roar, a wild grinding of the treads, and a hardly muffled curse from Hogan, the steel and iron Gargantua found a kind of footing in the wet uncertain road that was Hemlock Creek.

The strange partnership of Hansen and Hogan—and, invisibly, Angie Skykomish—was bringing out pulpwood logs for the second day of its existence. Off the mouth of the creek, down on the rugged coast of the Peninsula, there'd be another tug. She'd be standing by to make up another raft, ready to tow it north around Cape Flattery, through the Juan de Fuca Strait, then southward again into Tacoma.

Those four big babies behind the tractor would be sawed into bolts, chewed into tiny chips, then "cooked" with chemicals and steam to make the wood cellulose pulp that would in turn make paper.

But Carl Hansen was not thinking of these things. For weeks and months now he had dreamed of them; he had eaten them and slept them. Now they were reality and for the moment he had almost forgotten them.

His big browned hands were at Nadine's slender waist, steadying her on the quaking, jerking tractor seat. Her woman's warmth seeped through into his blunt and calloused fingers, and the perfume of her hair and skin mixed excitingly with the smells of cedar and spruce and the lofty lush needles of hemlocks.

Now Hansen was conscious only of these. And in his mind was a long memory of youth—of the awesome beauty of the Enchanted Valley, where men said the waterfalls numbered three thousand if you had the time and patience and strength to count them all. . . .

When the trio reached the coast camp at the mouth of the creek, Woody and Carl unchained the load and stowed the heavy links and tongs in the tractor box for the next trip.

"Well," Hogan said, stretching a grimy paw at his partner, "I still ain't sayin' I approve of what you propose to do, but good luck anyhow."

Hansen laughed, but kept his thumbs firmly hooked into his belt. "We're not saying good-by quite yet, Woody. I want you to drive us down to the Hoh Ranger Station, so you can bring the rig back here. You might have a tractor breakdown and need to get into town to order some parts. I don't want to put the roustabout out of commission for a week by parking it at Hoh."

Woodpecker Hogan growled like a timber wolf with its teeth on a wild hare. "That's downright thoughtful of you, son, but I'm cock-burned if I want to spend the rest of my natural life bein' a danged cho-*fure* for a couple of tourist hikers!"

"It's a nice little drive to Hoh," Hansen suggested persuasively. "And right now you haven't got a damned thing to do but sit on a rock and watch for the tug."

Nadine came to Carl's aid. "Anybody who can handle a tractor the way you do, Mr. Hogan, must be a wonder behind the wheel of a car."

Hogan glanced sidewise at her and Carl could almost see the jagged ice melting. But Hogan couldn't resist one shot in defeat. The old codger pulled his hard hat down over his eyes and stalked off toward the Ford roustabout. Over his shoulder he said, "And you figure Carl ain't exactly a safe driver? Does seem like I heard he's inclined to run off to the side of the road."

Hansen flushed and started after Hogan, but Nadine laid a restraining hand on his arm. "No, Carl," she whispered, laughing up at him quietly. "Woody's entitled to that. I did let myself in for it."

"The damned old coot," muttered Carl. "He ought to have his neck wrung out."

But he accepted Nadine's charitable mood. As they followed Hogan to the utility truck, it occurred to Carl that there was even subtle warning in Hogan's crack about driving off the road. It was a reminder that in and around Illahute, nobody ever forgot anything. Not even the ones you could call old friends.

Nadine and Hansen tossed their trail packs into the wide steel box of the roustabout and climbed into the cab beside Hogan. The latter had already whirled the starter, and Hansen and Nadine were hardly settled on the cushion when he spun the vehicle around into the side trail that would take them to U.S. Highway 101.

Hogan, still bristling, throttled wide to propel the little truck over the rise that stood between them and the highway beyond. There was no reason for him to glance at the rear-vision mirror.

If he *had* glanced into that little mirror his sharp eyes would have caught something to make him bring the roustabout to a screaming halt. For just as the little truck was disappearing over the hill, Angie Skykomish broke into the creek bank from the trail to Illahute.

At sight of the racing roustabout she waved frantically with both arms, a gesture desperate but unseen. At the same time she shouted at the top of her lungs—not the scream of a woman, but deep from her blood an Indian yell meant to pierce the forests. Yet it was unheard in the noisy cab of the roustabout.

Wild and unthinking in her desperation, Angie ran toward the narrow dirt road, clear to the top of the rise, where she shouted and waved again. But the little truck careened onward.

Angie Skykomish sank down, her knees buckling under the long run from town, her chin on her breast in tired frustration. She was crying angrily now, and it was as well that she did not lift her face toward the sky over Illahute. For there she would have seen the first trail of dark smoke that meant a fire had broken out in that little wooden town—a fire in the Golden Slipper.

Chapter Eleven

CARL HANSEN's prediction about Pete Baker was correct. The fat of Pete's high-school days was gone, and the man who welcomed Nadine and Carl as old friends was a hard and stocky ranger from the crown of his stiff-brimmed Stetson to the scarred toes of his trail boots.

When Hogan had taken his leave and nosed the roustabout toward the coast camp of Hansen and Hogan, the ranger ushered Nadine and Carl proudly into the sizable cedar-shake house that served as headquarters for that station area. A comfortable blaze was lively in the stone fireplace. Baker shoved a small table in front of the hearth and brought a steaming coffeepot and heavy cups and saucers.

Carl glanced around the big high-vaulted room. "This looks like the life, Pete."

The ranger laughed. "For a bachelor, I guess it's O.K. Keeps a man busy more than most folks realize. Right now I'm alone here. My assistant, Bromley, is on sick leave, and Herb Fenner is out on the trail trying to find a couple of dumb tenderfeet two days overdue."

Hansen waved toward the huge map on one wall. The area under the protection of government rangers, the deep wild heart of the Peninsula, was shaded in pink, and the trails, the stations, the fire lookouts, and the scattered shelter camps were sharply marked. "Nadine hasn't seen the Enchanted Valley. That's where we plan to head."

Baker looked at Hansen studiously but without alarm. "You'd have a closer chance at that if you came in from the southeast, along the Quinault. But I don't need to tell *you* that, Carl."

Hansen nodded agreement. "I figured we'd have a look at the White and Blue Glaciers, then cut across to the Hayes River trail and cut down again along Goodbin Creek to the Valley. On two legs of that trip there aren't any trails. Not even a foot trail—unless you've cut some in while I've been away."

Baker shook his head, looking at the big map. "We haven't." He turned to them and grinned. "Looks like you want to do it the hard way." His glance focused on Nadine. "Well, I'm not too worried about Carl trying that. Seems to me he knew his way around in there before I got into the ranger service."

"Then we don't have to get a green light from the chief of rangers?" Hansen asked.

Pete Baker stirred his coffee. "I didn't say anything like that. All I know is that tomorrow morning you're taking the trail to Blue Glacier. The trail ends at the glacier and there's a shelter there." Baker shrugged. "In a few days you don't show up here again. So probably I'll radiophone the ranger at Hayes River or Staircase that about then you ought to be hitting their trails."

"That won't make them very happy, will it?"

"Rangers can't be happy all the time," said Pete. "You got lost, that's all. You wandered off my trail and into theirs."

Carl smiled at Nadine. "I knew we could count on Pete. That's why I didn't want to go in anywhere but here at Hoh River."

Baker wagged a warning forefinger at them. "My friends, if anything happens to you, it will be my bones rotting in the rain as well as yours. Without an official O.K. from headquarters, I've never encouraged anybody to skip the trails, and I doubt I ever will again. What I ought to do is sing you a ranger song about getting off the trail."

Smiling, Baker took down a guitar from a peg on the wall. "Listen to this."

> "Mr. Rover Le Frapp
> Had no use for a map,
>   And never would stay on the path.
> He loved to jaywalk,
> But trails made him balk,
> And a guide just inspired his wrath."

Adjusting the guitar with dramatic air, Pete went on in the face of their laughter:

> "One morn in the wood
> All alone he did stood,
>   And started out yod'ling refrains;
> Disappeared in the wilds,
> Into miles of square miles,
> They never did find his remains!

"See that it doesn't happen to you," Pete said, replacing the guitar. He turned from the wall, facing Nadine, and a curious, embarrassed expression crossed his tanned features. Hansen, watching it, had been aware that Nadine had stopped laughing at the second verse. It was too reminiscent of what had happened to Johnny Wade. Carl felt sorry both for her and for the hapless but well-meaning Pete, who unwittingly had stumbled into the old memory of her father.

That night, after Nadine had retired early in the guest room, Pete was apologetic. "I knew I'd pulled a boner when I was halfway through the damned song. But I figured it would make things worse if I stopped."

"Forget it," Hansen advised. "Nadine will."

Baker looked oddly at Hansen. The ranger's face was a study of mixed emotions in the waning firelight. "Is that the reason she wants to go clear inside?" he asked slowly. "I mean—because the old man was lost in there?"

Carl nodded. "I think that's part of it. She told me she's always had a feeling Johnny Wade might still be alive."

Baker's whole body jumped in the rustic rocker and he was staring at Carl with such wide eyes that the logger said, "What the hell's biting you, Pete?"

The ranger got up and walked to the fireplace. He knocked the ashes from his pipe and laid it on the mantelpiece. Then he turned to Hansen. "They say there's a wild man back inside, you know."

"I didn't know. That is, I haven't run across the story since I've been back. But I remember there was always some such yarn, off and on, long before Johnny disappeared."

Baker shook his head. "I remember those stories. Sometimes they were just stories, made up by guides or hunters. And once in a while a 'nature man' would go back inside with nothing but a loincloth. That was usually for publicity and would turn out to be a fake. And sometimes a scared tenderfoot would mistake a grizzled settler for a wild man."

Hansen grinned. "Yeah. I guess the 'Old Man of the Hoh'—the guy who used to walk inside with a stove on his back and a sack of flour inside the stove—he's been taken for a wild man more than once."

Baker didn't answer for a long moment. Then he said,

"This report seems to be different, Carl. I heard it first about a year or so after Wade disappeared. To tell you the truth, I never did connect it with Johnny Wade until tonight. Until I sang that silly song and noticed that expression on Nadine's face. And now you tell me she believes he's alive."

"I didn't say she believed it. She's just got a feeling about it. You know how that goes, Pete. It happened in the war all the time. If a mother or sister or sweetheart didn't actually *see* the body—" He broke off, thinking about what Baker had said. Then he asked, "Just what makes this story different from the other wild-man yarns we used to hear?"

Baker looked a little nonplused at this direct question. His answer was somehow hesitant and he smiled sheepishly. "Well, maybe it only seems different to me, now that I'm in the service and realize how possible it is. A tough character with a certain hodgepodge of knowledge and some experience in the woods could survive back inside like a native in the African bush. And be just as private about it, if he wanted to keep out of sight."

Hansen nodded thoughtfully. "I think you're right, Pete."

"He might survive even without a weapon or tool to start out with," Baker went on. "But if he had a jackknife or even a small pocket knife, it would be the same as being born rich in a big city."

"Not for everybody, though. But for a guy like Johnny Wade . . ."

Baker's eyes grew round with excitement. "That's just it. A guy like Wade." He glanced at the closed door of the guest room where Nadine slept, remembered to keep his voice low. "They claim Johnny was a little off his rocker when he disappeared, from worry about the business or some family trouble or something. Being off the beam a bit could help rather than hinder in a situation like that. The less complicated a man was, the better off he might find himself. He'd be right down to primitive instincts—to the animal business of self-preservation, getting food, attacking and defending, keeping warm and dry and out of sight—"

Hansen cut him off impatiently. "If he wasn't off his nut to that extent when he went in, he'd be at that stage before long." The logger got up from his chair and

walked slowly to the wide window that looked toward
the black, jagged peak of Mount Olympus, the giant of
the Peninsula range. Turning to Baker, he said, "But
who's *seen* this wild man, or what evidence is there?"

"I don't go too much on the evidence," Pete answered
after a moment. "But when one or two dependable people claim to have glimpsed the guy—why, then, of course,
you begin to take some stock in the evidence."

"Do you happen to know anybody who thinks he's seen
the wild man?"

Baker nodded slowly. "Yes. Young Fenner, the fellow
who's out on the trail now. He's new in the service, and
very new to the Peninsula, so to tell you the truth, I
haven't taken much stock in his story until—well, until
today, when I sang that song and you and Nadine made
me remember Wade's disappearance."

"What did Fenner think he saw?"

As he asked the question Hansen dropped into his
chair again and lit a cigarette with irritation. The turn
of the talk with Baker made him somehow uncomfortable. If there was the ghost of a chance that Nadine's
hunch was right, that Johnny Wade was alive in the rain
forest, then Carl Hansen's conscience would make him
search. And deep within that conscience would be the
recollection that Hansen himself had upset Johnny Wade
badly—long before Jake Murchison appeared on the Illahute scene.

Yes, Johnny's only daughter, his only child, had been
the apple of his eye. So who could say for certain that
Wade's confusion hadn't begun on the very night young
Carl had brought her home to hostility and disgrace?
Maybe I softened him up for what Murchison was about
to do to him, Hansen thought.

It was a new thought to Carl, not a pleasant one; and
this talk of Pete Baker's had begun it. Carl hadn't
planned on this; all he had wanted was to show Nadine
the Enchanted Valley, to help her escape momentarily
the aftermath of her quarrel with her mother, the growing breach between her and this man Murchison. But if
Johnny Wade was really back inside . . .

Hansen exhaled a quick pillar of smoke and said
quickly, "Well? Don't be so damned mysterious, Pete.
What did Fenner think he saw?"

Baker drew a long breath. "Fenner was riding trail

just south of the shelter at the foot of Dodger Peak. In there the main trail joins up with the Press Valley trail, where you plan to hit after you skirt the foot of the glaciers. But off that is a mile or so of dead-end trail that stops at the base of Ludian Peak."

The ranger paused a moment. Then: "Riding trail, we don't usually bother about that little dead end if it's off season in the woods. But Fenner remembers distinctly a feeling that he ought to have a look down there. It's one of those hunches a guy can't exactly explain. Anyway, he was clear at the end of the dead-end trail and was wheeling his horse around when out of the corner of an eye—he said an inch or two would have put the whole thing clear out of his vision—he saw the brush move."

Baker hurried on. "It moved as if somebody or something had come part way out, then stepped back quickly. And behind the leaves, for just an instant, Fenner had an impression of a man's skin. You know, not white exactly, but still not the hide of any animal known in these parts."

"And that's all?"

"That's all," said Baker reluctantly. "Naturally, he didn't want to charge the horse into that brush, so Fenner did what you or I would have done. He slipped off his mount and tried to trail it. Something had gone through there, all right. But it wasn't a spot for footprints."

Hansen grunted. "The horse didn't shy or get nervous?"

The ranger grinned approvingly. "I was about to mention that, Carl. It didn't. And if there had been an animal in that brush, it would have."

"Still, it could have been the wind, moving the brush. What he thought was human skin could have been a glimpse of birch bark as Fenner wheeled the horse."

"Could have been, but Fenner was so sure it wasn't that he hobbled his horse a quarter mile away, came back to the spot on foot, and squatted there until nearly noon next day. There was a spring nearby and he thought maybe the guy—if it *was* a guy—would come back. But no luck."

Hansen was silent for several minutes while Pete slowly and methodically refilled his pipe. Then he laughed quietly, got up, and stretched himself. "Pete, if you figured to keep me awake tonjght, you wasted your time."

Baker looked at him oddly. "If I were in your boots, Carl, it wouldn't be yarns of wild men that would keep me awake. It would be the idea of acting as guide for a swell-looking dame like Nadine. What's your secret power, fellah?"

An incipient wave of anger rose in Carl, but he smothered it quickly. He realized that Pete meant nothing beyond a little kidding among old friends.

The logger grinned. "No secret to it, Pete. You might call it an old date that—well, that Korea interrupted."

Baker gave a mock sigh as he opened a door at the far end of the long room. "No girl like Nadine would keep a date with me that long. You're a lucky guy, Carl." The ranger motioned beyond the doorway. "You can take Fenner's bunk."

The mention of Fenner again brought the wild-man yarn to Hansen's mind. As he prepared for bed he found himself tense and wakeful, his brain racing with thoughts of Johnny Wade, of Sarah Wade, who had been a Baker-Smith, and of Jake Murchison, who by now might be spreading an alarm for Nadine.

He was up long before the gently snoring Pete Baker. Slipping quietly into the largest room of the ranger's cabin, he was startled to find Nadine, fully dressed, seated on the floor before the red glow of the crumbling logs in the fireplace. Her arms encircled her hunched-up knees. The smoke of a cigarette trailed upward from her fingers in the still air of the big room.

"I figured we ought to hit the trail early," Carl said quietly, "but not *this* early! Even the ranger is still sawing wood in there."

His voice, quiet as it was, shattered Nadine's calm. She leaped at once to her feet and turned to him half-smiling but somehow deadly serious. "Good morning, Carl. It seems to me I've been up for hours." She looked toward the window where the black was slowly bleaching into gray. "I walked outside a while," she added. "And I've got things ready to make breakfast. I thought maybe our host would like to get out of it for a change."

There was beneath the lightness of her tone an undercurrent he didn't like..Although she looked fresh and all her old vitality was apparent, Carl sensed she had slept but little. Something was wrong; and in the next instant he knew what it was.

"Carl, I—I've done some thinking, and I mustn't go back inside with you."

He felt himself recoiling as if from a blow. "But why? What's happened?"

She shook her head. "Nothing, except that I've begun to quiet down after that quarrel with Mother. I'm thinking straighter, and I must say that Woody Hogan's attitude helped wake me up. I've got to get back to town and face the music alone."

"I just don't get it," Hansen said heavily. "Yesterday . . ." His voice trailed into helpless silence.

"Don't you see, Carl? I can't do this to you. I'll only mean trouble for you, Carl."

"You've said that before, and it made no difference to me. It doesn't now. Nothing has changed."

"I've changed," Nadine said with that curious half-smile that always got deep inside him. "I'm not good for you, Carl. I never have been. And I never will be, until I get clear away from—from all that's been holding me. When I've done that, then maybe . . ." She did not finish, but the blue eyes were bright with hope and promise.

There was an old fear in them, too, that Carl recognized. It brought him to swift decision. He stepped forward and gripped her by the arms. "You'll never get clear unless I help you do it," he told her grimly. "And if trouble is coming, it's better that it come now. Better for all of us."

His fingers gripped her arms tighter; he almost shook her, with a kind of gentle ferocity, hardly knowing what he did. He went on in a husky whisper: "Nadine, we have to go back inside. Take my word for that."

He wanted to say more. He wanted to tell her how he, too, had spent a restless night, and why. He wanted to tell her of Fenner's experience. Yet he knew that it would be unfair, and could be tragic, to raise her hopes that her old feeling was right and Johnny Wade could be alive.

Then Pete Baker opened his bedroom door and saw them standing tense by the fireplace. Hansen stepped back guiltily from Nadine.

Nadine laughed lightly. "I was getting cold feet. I'm afraid your song unnerved me last night, Pete. But Carl has convinced me that"—her blue gaze turned steadily on Hansen—"you don't get as far as the Hoh and then turn back."

Carl's heart soared at the words, at the steady man-to-man gaze in his direction. He felt again that here was a woman for the woods, for a man who belonged to the woods. "And this girl is all set to make our breakfast," he told Pete proudly. "This morning you begin your duties as a man of leisure."

Obviously Pete was delighted. "While Nadine's slaving in the galley, come on out to the corral and I'll introduce you to Snoose, the best pack animal in the whole Olympic Peninsula."

Snoose was all his owner claimed—sleek black hide, small but rugged, and friendly in a knowing way. "I hate to take him away from you," Hansen said.

"You won't for long," Baker laughed. "You couldn't get him beyond the glaciers with all the sugar in the world. He knows it's no fit country for horses or man along Ice River. But he'll be a big help to you as far as the foot of Mount Olympus. You can cache some stuff at the shelter there, and Snoose will come back here along the trail at a jog, won't you, boy?" Snoose nuzzled Pete's shoulder in agreement.

After the hearty breakfast prepared by Nadine, the ranger guided them across the big station clearing to the start of the Hoh River trail. At the edge of the clearing the wall of the rain forest jutted upward abruptly. The station was at the periphery of an area that soaked up 130 inches of rain a year, more than most tropical regions of the North American continent.

But this morning was clear, and Nadine was happily surprised at the cheerful vista immediately ahead. Despite the dense tree canopy, the forest bottom appeared almost luminous.

"You've got a wonderful morning for a start," Pete Baker said jovially. "But I don't need to warn either of you that it can't last. The trail's about like this for ten or eleven miles. Remember, Carl? Then you begin to hit glacier and timberline country."

The ranger shook hands with them both. As they passed between the gray rustic posts that were the simple markers beginning the trail, he whacked the pack animal smartly on the flank. "Take good care of them, Snoose boy, and report back to me!"

Man, woman, and horse took to the narrow trail single file. In a matter of seconds they were lost to sight in the foliage. Smiling, the ranger turned and walked briskly back to the station cabin. There was work to do.

Inside the cabin he went first to the radiophone room to tune in for the fire reports. On the afternoon before, the lookout on Hurricane Hill had reported a smoke rise on the coast. He called the Soleduc Ranger Station to get the latest word.

"Building fire in Illahute," Soleduc reported. "Under control now. No forest damage, no lives lost, but building is complete loss. Anything else, Hoh?"

"What building?" Baker asked. "I'm from that town."

There was something like a smothered guffaw at Soleduc. "Condolence, then! It was the Golden Slipper!"

Pete signed off and flicked the switch. So the old Golden Slipper was no more! It had been a landmark in Illahute, and Pete figured Carl Hansen would certainly be interested to know about it.

The ranger hurried as far as the rustic posts marking the trail's beginning. He knew he could easily overtake the man and the girl and the pack animal now. But right there he stopped, grinning to himself ruefully.

"Take it slow, Baker, old boy," he muttered aloud. "With Nadine there with him, it wouldn't be smart to go thrashing up to Carl with news about the Golden Slipper, would it?"

Of course not, he answered himself, turning back to the cabin. And anyhow, what did a man hit the Peninsula trails for, if not to get away from news and civilization?

Chapter Twelve

FROM THE BIG BAY WINDOW of the Golden Slipper, Angie Skykomish had seen the tug dragging the first raft of Hansen and Hogan pulpwood logs northward toward Cape Flattery.

Her heart swelled at the sight, and the volatile mixture of French and Haida blood raced inside her supple brown body. It was not only because her savings were in the brash new outfit of Hansen and Hogan. There was in her elation a genuine pride in her old friends Carl and Woody. For to Angie, the young man returned and the old man nearly forgotten represented "her side" in the continuous battle of life in that microcosm of the world which was the shabby weathered town of Illahute.

As if in answer to her emotions, the tug signaled with a long piercing whistle as it came abeam of the town. Passing the old Baker-Smith and Wade wharves, almost empty now, their silent half-rusted loading cranes jutting skyward like skeletons of giants expired in violent struggle, the chugging Diesel tug plowed on north with its valuable tow.

The tug and raft had hardly become toys against the north horizon when Angie's old-fashioned hand bell whirred dully against the front door of the Golden Slipper. It was a strange hour for callers or prospective roomers. Out of ancient habit Angie pulled back the lace curtains an inch or two and peered onto the porch.

Her visitors were Buck Flack and Jake Murchison.

Angie's first instinct was to pretend that nobody was at home. But something in the outlines of the two men, something in the sagging grimness with which they glared at the door, advised her that silence would not deter their entrance. Besides, Angie Skykomish had not been designed by God or fashioned by experience to fear men.

She walked briskly to the front door, opened it wide, and bade them good morning in the clipped respectable tone of a respectable rooming-house keeper.

Obviously, Murchison was the boss here; but Flack was allowed to do the talking. "Mornin', Angie," Flack said with mock, sneering courtesy. "Wonder if you'd mind lettin' Mr. Hansen know he has visitors. I guess you met Mr. Murchison."

"Yes. But Carl isn't here. He's—" She stopped, closing her red lips into a thin line.

"Up Hemlock Creek doin' a little gyppo logging, eh?" Flack's sneer grew broader. "That's kind of what we thought, seeing the tug and raft go by. I guess that means Hogan ain't in, either."

"It does," Angie said, starting to shut the door. "I'm sorry. I'll tell them you called, if I see them."

"Just a minute, Angie honey!" Flack inserted a huge muddy boot between door edge and frame. 'We don't mind talkin' to you. Do we, Jake?"

Murchison tried to smile, but it was a twisted thing that could have as easily reflected agony or anger. "Not at all," he said.

Thinking quickly, Angie pretended to misunderstand. She smiled as pleasantly as she could manage. "You boys have had a little too much and too early. Lost your memories. There aren't any girls here now. There haven't been for some time."

"Hell, we know that," Flack said. "That is, we know there ain't no girl here but *you*, Angie. Nothing wrong with you, is there, Angie?"

"Just a minute, Flack," said Murchison, taking over now. His slitted glance went to Angie. "We want to talk about this Hansen and Hogan operation on Hemlock Creek."

Angie shook her head. "I don't know anything about that."

"We know you do," Murchison said. He nodded at Buck Flack. "Let's go inside."

Angie realized she couldn't keep them out now. She was alone in the house. For a fleeting desperate moment she thought of running to the wall phone to call the sheriff. But what good would it do to telephone Sheriff Hunsicker about a visit from Jake Murchison, who practically ran the town for Sarah Wade and Henry Baker-Smith? "If they ain't tearin' the joint down, Angie, what can I do? You got a public inn there, haven't you?" That's about what she'd get from Sheriff Hunsicker now.

She backed away from the door, leading the way into the rococo parlor. "How about a little drink, Angie?" Flack asked.

"I haven't any liquor in the house, Buck."

He grinned at Murchison, swaying. "Listen to that,

Jake! Pure as the drifted snow around here now!" There was heavy irony in the thickened words.

Murchison glared at Flack, his anger rising. "I didn't know it took so little whisky to make an idiot of you, Flack." He turned his sudden spleen on Angie. She recognized that Murchison had meant to keep control of himself, put the burden of any rough pressure on Flack. But Flack was confused; the past atmosphere of the Golden Slipper had returned to his alcoholized brain, and Angie knew he wanted her. Murchison saw it, too, and in anger was losing control of himself; he looked dangerous, almost evil. For the first time in her life Angie Skykomish was afraid of a man.

"Flack and his boys warned Hansen," he said through his teeth. "You and that senile fool Hogan were here. You heard the warning. But Hansen has gone ahead, and you and Hogan went along with him."

Angie had meant to be resilient if she could, but now fear made her defiant. "I don't speak for Woody Hogan. But all right, I did go along with Carl Hansen—and as far as I could. What of it?"

The words were hardly out of her mouth when she knew they were a ghastly error. Murchison went white. He half lunged, dizzily, then caught himself. The man is mad, Angie told herself in slow astonishment. He's crazy with frustration. For a long time now he's had control of old Sarah and old Henry and Nadine, and that meant he had control of everything around here. But now . . .

Murchison said, "To hell with Hogan and Hansen for now. Have you got Nadine here?"

"Nadine?" The question puzzled her.

"Nadine Wade, yes," Murchison said. He was growing whiter. He steadied himself against the battered oak table. To Flack he said, "If Nadine's not here now, she may show up here. She hasn't taken a car out of town, or the bus. That means she's either with Hansen at Hemlock Creek, or will show up here. There's no place else for her to go." Drawing an angry breath, he turned to Angie. "I'm leaving Flack here."

"No!" Angie flared, the hot mixed blood rushing to her face.

"I'm leaving Flack here," Murchison said, separating each word for Flack's benefit as well as hers. "And if he knows what's good for him, he'll stay until I let him off, and he won't let you out of his sight."

Buck Flack leaned back against the wall and laughed like a childish giant. "You bet I'll stay; Jake! You bet I won't let her out of my sight."

Angie's eyes flashed fire. "You do this, Jake Murchison, and—and I'll kill your man! I'll kill him!"

"You do and you'll hang." But Murchison stared at her, believing. He looked at Flack. "She'd do it, too. She'd slit your throat, you fool, if you dozed off once."

The inflamed logger roared again with laughter. "Who dozes off with Angie the squaw?"

Angie rushed, slapped him with all her strength across the bleared mouth. Then Murchison took her from behind. "We'd better strip her now," he breathed. "Make sure she doesn't have a knife. Then you get her into a room upstairs, lock the door, and, damn you, *stay* there!"

Buck Flack laughed again, drunk and insane with liquor and anticipation, holding Angie's thin wrists. "Ho, ho! Wait till the old lady hears about this! Wait till I don't get home and she finds out where I was. She'll burn the goddamn Golden Slipper down—just like she swore she'd do when we warned Hansen!"

Shivering, Angie Skykomish at least heard Murchison slam the front door. A key turned in the lock. She stopped struggling then, in the huge bear grip of Flack. It was foolish, she told herself bitterly; it was, of course, a thing to make this drunken brute laugh, as he laughed now between his hard breathing.

But there was another reason, and not a bitter, cynical one, for acting now what she once had been. It would be the only way to escape now. The only way. Suddenly she flashed her dark eyes on him. "Look, my huge friend. Now that Jake Murchison is gone, perhaps I could find that drink."

The blood-streaked eyes widened. "No tricks, Angie."

And he saw to it that there were no tricks. All that day and through the awful night, Buck Flack saw to that. And Murchison did not come back. No one came.

But Angie knew that Flack must sleep; he could not fight the liquor and his hot blood and his waves of weariness forever. Toward dawn he slept. Angie searched for the key and found it, let herself out of the upstairs room, dressed quickly, and ran blindly into the street.

Running as fast as she could, before the darkness lifted from the town to betray her, she headed into the winding foot trail above the beach. Lifting her skirts high, brown legs twinkling along the trail with the speed her mother's race knew, Angie Skykomish strained toward the mouth of Hemlock Creek.

Topping the rise on the north bank, she saw the bright scarred logs of spruce and hemlock that Carl and Woody had unchained a few moments before. She caught sight of the Ford roustabout on the side road leading to U.S. Highway 101. Hogan was at the wheel, Carl Hansen beside him, and a woman she knew must be Nadine, though the morning sun flashed on the windshield too quickly for sure identification. So Murchison's half-crazed suspicion had been right!

Angie shouted and waved. She started running again, but it was too late. She sank down exhausted, spent in every fiber from her nightmare with Flack and the race from Illahute. She burst into weary, angry tears, and collapsed full length until she too slept.

She did not hear the signal of the tug that dropped hook off Hemlock Creek, waiting for the make-up of the second Hansen and Hogan raft. Nothing but the roar of the other tractor, bouncing and jarring down the wet creek bed, brought Angie alive again.

Carl and Woodpecker and Johnny Wade's girl had taken the roustabout to the Hoh River Station, looked like, the tractor crew told Angie. Hogan was due to return, but not Carl, for a while. They heard he was guiding the Wade girl back inside.

By then the black smoke pillar had risen in the north, over Illahute. The crew speculated about that, but Angie knew in her heart it was the Golden Slipper. Buck Flack's "old lady" must have taken the drastic action she had promised.

Or maybe an enraged Murchison had set the torch—and seen to it that the groggy Flack was part of the flames. Angie shuddered. In any case, she felt sure, the blame would be put on Flack's wife.

But Angie held her tongue and waited for Hogan. When he returned he was surprised to find Angie there, but not at the news she brought him. "It's started, then," Hogan growled. "Quicker than we figured."

Woodpecker turned to the tractor crew. "Boys, when

you joined up, maybe you recollect Carl mentioning that some people—Buck Flack, for one—don't much like the idea we got here. He said we could be in for a little fracas, maybe. Well, Angie says it might be on the way now."

A big logger spat on both his palms, grinned, and took up his peavey like a weapon. "A little extra exercise never hurt a man none," he said, and the others laughed.

Hank, the redhead who had complained from his bunk the night before, moved a step toward Hogan and the girl. "What you're tellin' us—would *that* be why Hansen lit out so quick this morning?"

Angie's temper was faster than Hogan's. She lifted her small brown face to the logger's. "You're a stranger in these parts, or I'd know you," she said evenly. "Also you'd know Carl Hansen better. Maybe you will yet if he finds out what you think of him."

Hank looked down at the fiery eyes, faintly amused. "Seems like this show is overrun with dames. Who the hell bought *you* into the outfit?"

Now Woody Hogan stepped up shoulder to shoulder with the breed girl. "Angie bought herself in, with her own money. She's comin' back to Hemlock camp with us." He glared at the lot of them, his cantankerous old eyes narrowed. "All you brush monkeys remember she's one of the bosses in this outfit, *and* to be treated like such!"

The rangy Hank squinted down at Angie with new respect, and with something else in his eyes—something he could not have defined himself just then. "That's *copacete* with me," he said slowly, using the Chinook jargon for "very good." "*Hiyu muckamuck copacete.*"

Angie Skykomish flushed darkly, lowering her gaze. This tall redheaded stranger know nothing about her; he saw her only as she stood, and he liked her. That much was plain to Angie. It was in the redhead's laughing eyes.

Chapter Thirteen

To Nadine the first half mile of the twisting Hoh River trail was a sight for open-mouthed wonder.

Those two rustic posts behind her and Carl marked more than the begining of a trail. They marked, as well, the western boundary of the rain forest—a meandering line almost as visible as though it had been a wall. Here the trees were suddenly different in their aspect, and so was the crowded floor of the forest. It was not simply vastness, not mere complexity and jungle tangle. For the moment there was no rain; the atmosphere was green bright cut through with shafts of pale yellow. Nonetheless, the feel and the look here was sharply tropical— lush, steaming, filled with a thousand unseen eyes and with a thousand tiny indistinguishable sounds that, paradoxically, created a kind of universal silence that struck awe into the girl's breast.

The trio skirted the Hoh at the start of their journey. Carl was in the lead, and the amiable Snoose picked his way delicately behind Nadine. Hansen held his runt machete in readiness, but only occasionally did he chop at a bough or bramble across the trail to make the way easier for Nadine. The trail here was well marked, narrow but open, suitable enough for mount or foot travel.

Nadine could not help noticing the quiet, relaxed ease with which Carl moved. His gait and carriage reminded her of the walk of Indians she had seen along the coast. The machete seemed almost tiny in his big fist; the pack sat lightly behind shoulders whose muscles rippled beneath his shirt as he swung along. She had confidence in his easy stride, almost slow, and designed, she suspected, to get there on the long pull. On this morning, unusually clear, she could now and then glimpse the snow-streaked tower of Mount Olympus. But Carl said its lower slopes, where White and Blue Glaciers moved with geologic slowness, were nearly twenty miles distant.

As they moved along, the trail became all but invisible except for the ground beneath their feet. The green world closed in behind them as they moved; ahead of them it opened momentarily, only a little at a time. It's like a sea, Nadine thought, a great green sea. It comes at you like the combers; it thrusts around you, and over you, and under you, and only now and then can you see the sky.

When the sun stood overhead they stopped to eat.

"There's a spring over there," Carl said. He chose for their tablecloth a carpet of greenery surrounded by bracken and moss fern. The place was shaded by the great upturned roots of a fallen hemlock. The twining roots, matted with damp black soil out of which sword fern grew, formed a sheltering wall. The bright flames of a patch of wild tiger lilies flared up beyond the rotted log.

Dropping the saddle pack on the mossy floor, Hansen guided Snoose to a spot of grazing meadow. It had been browsed down by roaming elk, Hansen noted. But Snoose was an old hand at foraging behind the hungry herds, making the most of any mountain grass patch.

Nadine and Carl lunched frugally too. Hard biscuit, a bar of chocolate for energy, and half a can of Army rations—beef chunks, cold potatos and carrots, powdered lemonade made in a tin cup filled with water from the cold spring. "We'll make the heavy meal at sundown, and try for good breakfasts," Carl said.

She sighed, glancing happily around them. "I feel very complete," she said, and lay back on the mossy carpet, shielding her eyes from a shaft of light that filtered down.

Complete. Carl thought it an odd word with which to say she wasn't hungry. Yet it was the right word, too—because, he felt sure, she meant more than that, whether she realized it or not.

She lay as gracefully relaxed as a tawny lioness. The full red lips were parted slightly, as if she might have dropped asleep. Her measured breathing was marked by the rise and fall of her breasts beneath the crimson woodsman's shirt. He could see a hint of their whiteness where the tan of her throat stopped.

"You can keep the rain away from me, Carl."

The words, whispered so urgently, came back to him with such force that he thought for a moment he had heard them again. His glance darted at the red lips; they were motionless.

Don't keep watching her, he told himself. See how Snoose is doing; take a walk up the trail; let her sleep. If you don't . . . He turned away again, trying to concentrate on how the elk had nubbed down the shrubs, trying to pick out their footprints at the base of the tangled mass. If it was this bad already, he thought, how would it be at the shelters, with the night shutting out the world? With only the girl and himself, together in as much of the world as could be lit by a tiny fire?

Suddenly from somewhere close came a prolonged quavering sound, almost as of escaping steam. It was a drawn-out, musical hiss, repeated now on a lower pitch. The girl sat upright, eyes round and questioning. Hansen laughed shortly. Getting to his feet, he extended his hand to help her up, "The varied thrush," he said. "Doesn't let himself be seen much, but you can hear him plenty."

"I must have dozed," Nadine said.

The spell was broken. Carl's tone was more brusque than he intended. "The nights are for sleeping. We'd better get on." He picked up the saddle pack and was moving toward the grass where Snoose now was blowing playfully.

Puzzled, and not a little shocked, Nadine stared at Carl's retreating back. His swift change troubled and hurt her. She wondered if already he regretted his absence from the Hemlock Creek activities. Maybe he was missing the crusty Hogan, or—this struck with sudden chill—Angie, the strangely pretty girl of French and Haida blood who, everyone said, had more than one kind of interest in the outfit called Hansen and Hogan.

Or had Carl suddenly recalled the night her father offered her in marriage—but only providing Carl put himself in the hands of the Wades and Baker-Smiths, only if he admitted tacitly that he was not yet fit even to look at Nadine Wade?

Nadine could hardly be expected to know the very simple truth of Carl's queer mood. There was no way yet for her to understand completely how he wanted her in every rough fiber of his being, yet how something kept telling him she was not what he should have, not what was good for him. Nadine herself had suggested as much.

As he moved into the trail with the pack horse she said quietly, "It's only half a day from the ranger station. Are you sure we should go on?"

He looked up, surprised. He understood how abrupt

and surly he had been. The darknes swept from his face as though he moved from shadow into sunlight. "We promised ourselves once . . . remember?"

For that was part of Carl Hansen, too. A man dreamed a dream. He made promises, to himself, to others. So that sometime . . .

The first trail shelter was like the rest, Hansen said.

It was part log cabin and part lean-to, with a slanting plane for a roof, and open on the weather side. There were pallets on which to spread sleeping bags or blankets. There was a small shovel hanging on a peg, and above it ranger's orders to bury garbage.

There was even firewood, stacked neatly by the iron stove, but Carl ignored that. He gathered deadwood and down branches. He knew that others might reach the shelter in far less fortunate weather. He knew they might reach it in illness, or in injury, or in sheer tenderfoot panic long after darkness had fallen.

On the second night, still skirting the Hoh and climbing steadily, they ignored the shelter altogether. Hansen built a small fire in a clearing. They made their supper over that, and left it glowing when they stretched beneath the cedars in their sleeping bags. "There'll be no shelters soon," Carl said, "and I want to break you in."

Her eyes flashed with humor. "I'm not complaining."

He looked at her with admiration. No, she hadn't complained. She was good on the trail. His hunch about her had been right, and this made him feel good. A man likes to have his judgment vindicated, especially about a woman.

The next day the trail veered sharply south, and Mount Olympus seemed close enough to reach out and touch. They could feel the tang of the glaciers on the late-afternoon air as they approached a ranger shelter.

When Hansen stopped, Nadine wanted to press on. "I'm really not tired," she said, "and we seem so near the mountain."

He laughed. "Good girl. But people have been tricked on distances before in this light. And even if you're not tired yet, tomorrow we rest until noon."

"Then I want a bath," Nadine said.

"The Hoh isn't much of a tub up here," he told her. "And Glacier Creek is even less satisfactory. Tomorrow

we ought to hit Elk Lake. You can thrash around in that."
He paused, smiling. "I might join you, if it's not too
cold."

"So?"

At the questioning monosyllable Hansen burst into
laughter. His spirits had vastly improved since that noon
of the first day on the trail. The cloak of civilization was
almost off his shoulders now. Except for his common-
sense caution on the trail and in camp, he began to experience a feeling of recklessness, of being subject to no
more than the commandments of the rangers in these
wilds.

"No hunting, no disturbing of wildlife, no injury to
the vegetation—and thou shalt not take short cuts across
switchbacks on the trails," he recited to Nadine that night
as they sat staring into the fire. "That's all the regula-
tion we need to worry about here. Pretty simple, eh?"

She had lit a cigarette, but after only a puff or two she
turned to him and put it between his lips. "Funny . . .
I don't feel like smoking much up here. And I was getting so I was breaking into a second pack every day."

"You're unwinding too," he said. Inhaling deeply on
the cigarette, he was conscious of a faint and sweet perfume in it—a delicate and strangely moving scent.

"Papa used to get very angry at the ranger service, you
know," she said after a moment. "He said they would
only make a useless park out of this. But now I understand what they really do—they keep it rugged and wild
the way it's always been."

Carl nodded. "That's right. You know, every damned
thing here, even the wood mice and the insects, the cougars as well as the elk—those dead, rotting trees as well
as the living ones—they all affect each other, they're all
part of the whole shebang. Destroy one thing and you
hurt all the rest some way."

Nadine was looking at him strangely, fondly. "That's
queer talk for a logger, Carl. I never heard Papa or Uncle Henry talk that way."

"Maybe not. But you can bet Hogan and I are going
to remember it. For every damned tree we take off Hemlock, there's going to be at least two come up."

Her gaze was still steady, faintly amused and somehow
proud. "You're a lot different from the Carl Hansen I
first knew," she said slowly.

He spun the stub of the cigarette into the fire and turned to face her in the pink glow. "Did you like the other one better?" he asked.

She shook her head, smiling. "Not better, perhaps. But I did like him, Carl. Very much." It was quiet, straightforward, he thought, like all the rest of her. There was a meaning here, unmistakable, which he could take or leave, as he chose. There was a long silence, and then she added, "You were the first, Carl. Afterward, when you'd gone, I wondered if you knew that. I—I sort of wanted you to know it."

There was a strangeness in the way she said it that held him from taking her in his arms as he wanted. "I knew it," he said.

She did not answer, but the strangeness was still there; it was in her eyes now instead of in her voice. It was around them in the fire glow; a strangeness that was crazily sweet and sad. Suddenly he knew what she was trying to tell him. He said dully, and the voice seemed not quite to be coming from him: "I wasn't the last. Naturally. You—you're too damned beautiful for anyone to expect that . . ."

His voice trailed into nothingness and suddenly the vision of Murchison rose between them. He saw the flicker of hurt in her eyes, but her gaze never flinched from his own.

No, Hansen thought painfully, there hadn't been several men, or three or two, since that murky Sunday when Johnny Wade blessed them with his fancy Packard, then cursed them in white-hot anger. There'd been but one; only Murchison. *Only* Murchison!

He stood up, red anger flooding his vision. He almost stepped into the fire on his blind way into the darkness. She leaped to her feet, followed to the edge of the firelight, then stopped, hearing his heedless threshing through the brush. The sounds of his angry striding seemed to come from all around her. She cried out his name just once, and then there was silence; the unbelievable silence of the rain forest in the dead of night, an oppressive silence that is more than absence of sound—that is in reality the continuous crashing thunder of the gods of Mount Olympus, the grinding of the gears of the universe.

She had no way of knowing that Carl's anger was not

for her, that it was for Murchison and his evil hold on her and all the Wades. She couldn't realize that he held her blameless, or that despite this, the crimson anger spent all his wild desire in a flash.

Turning back toward the fire, Nadine dropped to her knees before it, tears glistening on her smooth cheeks. The hot glow of the fire dried the tears. Slowly there flooded into the strong slender body its own kind of anger—an anger that was mostly a woman's hurt for the things that might have been, and the things she could not help now, no matter where her heart lay.

When Carl Hansen returned to the shelter with the faint pink shafts of eastern sun rising over Olympus, she was gone.

He stood there dazed, trying to return to a kind of thinking consciousness that had somehow left him in his madness of the night before. He could not have said whether he walked the trail all night, returning to the camp with blind subconscious effort, or whether he had finally slept exhausted, or only sat staring at the darkness, his brain crawling with the desire to destroy Murchison and all the man meant.

It did not matter now. Nadine was gone.

He called, and waited, without answer. Her name echoed back, eerily repeated. His hoarse, frightened voice ricocheted in and out among the great trees, mocking him through the pale gray-green light of early morning.

He looked in the shelter. Her pack was gone; so was the light silk-down sleeping bag he had spread on the pallet as they unpacked for the night. Frantically but carefully he examined the trail along which they had come. For three or four hundred yards he bent along it, straining for some sign that could mean she had gone back along that way. Surely she had decided that she could only go back—that he wanted nothing of her now, Murchison's woman. At least, Hansen thought bitterly, she could feel there was need for her in Illahute, however twisted and strange that need might be, however tragic in the end.

But the weather had been dry and the trail was thin and powdery now, difficult to read with any certainty. He could barely discern where the two of them and Snoose had traveled upward.

Slowly he went back to the dying fire, poked up the coals, and set the already half-filled coffeepot over them. Squatting stiffly on his haunches, he rubbed a hand over his unshaven face. It felt leathery, taut, and his lips were dry. There were tiny pin points of pain at his forehead and temples. He felt, he thought wryly, as if he had been drunk the whole night.

That reminded him of the sealed pint of whisky in the saddle pack. He could use some of that now. Taking it from the pack, he thumbed open the seal and poured whisky carelessly into the now bubbling coffeepot. The fumes of the stale coffee and the whisky were not pleasant in the chill dawn. But after he had swallowed some of the liquid from a tin cup he no longer minded the smell.

"Coffee royal!" He laughed half aloud, sardonically. "Coffee royal in the shadow of Mount Olympus!"

Was he drunk already? Hot spiked coffee on an empty stomach could be powerful.

He laughed again, then stopped suddenly and compressed his lips into a thin angry line. Quit kidding yourself, he whispered. Nothing's wrong with you except Nadine. She's gone.

He started to pour a little more from the pint into the coffee. Instead, he lifted the bottle quickly away and screwed the cap tight. Returning it to the saddlebag he was conscious of something gone from the pack. For a minute or two he could not recall what was missing. Then he knew. It was the map of the Peninsula. He had carried it in his shirt pocket the first day, but it got too damp with sweat and he'd put it in the saddle pack. Now it was gone.

Of course it was gone. Nadine had taken it!

He stood up, smiling, the lines in his face erasing a little. She'd gone on. He'd been a fool not to surmise that. She might believe he didn't want her around; she might be angry and hurt; but she wouldn't go back now. There in Pete's cabin she had said, "Carl's convinced me you don't get as far as the Hoh and turn back."

But that map wouldn't do her much good beyond the glaciers. He could find it useful after the Hoh trail petered out, but not someone who hadn't been back inside many times.

He lifted his face to the sun, a washed-out yellow behind the haze. It was higher than he would have believed.

Hurrying now, he moved toward Snoose, the saddle pack in his hand. Nadine had several hours' start on him now. And she'd be moving fast—probably too damned fast for her own good, because she was angry and hurt.

As he led Snoose back to the trail he stopped dead still, looking down at a soft patch in the grove of alders where the animal had grazed. What he saw seemed fresh, and very much like the print of a foot.

But it had been a strange foot, if that was what it was. Hansen knelt to look closer. It seemed hardly the print of a man, nor yet of an animal. Still, it could have been made by a human foot in—Hansen felt his breath catching —in a very badly made mocassin or hide wrapping.

There was one other, not far off, in a wet spot where water was seeping up from under the ground. Then no others. The ground was hard elsewhere, covered with matted needles and dry rusty moss. Hansen stood up, his face grave. He started for the trail, yanking taut the line around Snoose's neck, surprising the easygoing animal.

As Carl Hansen moved southeast and deep into the Hoh River trail, he remembered the story Herb Fenner had brought back to Pete Baker from the base of Ludden Peak. He lifted his face toward Olympus, whose black and white peak was like a jagged blade at the gray throat of the sky. His face was lifted there with a hope that was almost like a prayer to the gods of the mountain.

If those prints were actually those of Fenner's "wild man," then Carl hoped the man was indeed Johnny Wade.

And, he hoped, a Johnny Wade whose mind was in balance.

Chapter Fourteen

BY MIDAFTERNOON Hansen had skirted the base of Mount Carrie, where the Hoh bent sharply from its source. Still he had not overtaken Nadine or glimpsed any sign of her passage along the trail.

He and the pack animal were heading almost due south now. Olympus, king of all the peaks, loomed nearly straight ahead. The air was sharper, more rarefied, the vegetation was a little less tangled and complex, the trees showed the effects of altitude and wind. He should be reasonably close to the timber line by nightfall.

Far off to his right, to the westward, squall clouds were gathering darkly. But they were very far off; perhaps forty or fifty miles. It was hard to judge, but certainly they were over the Pacific, farther away than Hoh Head and the rugged rock islands scattered along the coast. And they might drop their heavy load of water long before reaching the Olympics. No weather prediction could be made safely on such clouds now.

Hansen wished they were closer. Paradoxically, he had begun to curse the fair weather. The trail was too packed and hard and dry to allow him to distinguish Nadine's footprints from a dozen other less recent disturbances on the path. Each mile now weakened his certainty that he was on the trail ahead. A dozen times or more he wished for a cloudburst or swift mountain shower that would show her presence unmistakably between him and the glaciers.

As he moved along the trail without sight or sign of Nadine, his certainty of her direction was further jarred by the vision of those queer footprints near the last shelter. Once, in his anxiety to increase his pace, he tried Snoose as a mount. But the little animal had never been broken, apparently, to saddle or bareback. Carl found he could make the maximum progress by adding his own pack to Snoose's load and then urging the animal as fast as possible ahead of him. Snoose was unhappy at this tactic, as well, but there was no alternative.

Carl remembered that nightfall should bring him to a shelter that rangers called Chicago for identification purposes. It was the only shelter between him and Elk Lake, the next to the last on the Hoh River trail. A few miles beyond the lake the trail ended, except for that mile or two of dead-end trail toward Ludden Peak, where Fenner believed he saw the wild man of the Olympics. And Hansen hoped against hope that he'd find Nadine camped at Chicago. Unless she had started out well before dawn, he did not see how she could have got farther.

As the afternoon light weakened, Snoose found himself pressed to a faster and faster pace. The closer Carl moved toward Olympus and the dusk, the less confident he became that Nadine would be found at the shelter. He was prepared when a bend in the trail at last revealed the shelter—empty. Its tiny stone chimney was innocent of wood smoke; the ashes in the iron stove were cold. There was no indication anywhere that the shelter had been used in recent weeks.

Hansen's first inclination was to push on, meeting the gathering darkness on the trail. But a man struggling along the trail at night could miss a lot of things, even though he was sure he could follow the way. He might miss something far more important than the few miles gained by night travel, always risky. And now Carl was less sure than ever that Nadine was ahead of him. Perhaps she had turned back, after all. Perhaps—and he did not like this thought—she was not on the trail at all.

He relieved Snoose of the packs and set the animal to grazing. Carl was not hungry, but forced himself to eat a cold meal. For the first time on the trail he felt chilled, felt the night winds from the glaciers and the snow-capped peaks filtering through his clothes. He wanted hot coffee badly, but even more he wanted no telltale fire at the shelter tonight. Not until morning, or until he had found Nadine safe, or an explanation for those strange formless footprints in the forest meadow.

He wanted most of all to think, and as the night closed in he sat on one of the hard pallets in the shelter without unpacking his sleeping bag. He felt tired, and very sleepy, but he figured that the chill would keep him awake.

It did not. When he opened his eyes he knew the morning was about to break. He was hunched into a ball on the pallet, knees against his chest, and shivering. The outline of Mount Olympus was barely visible. A bird or two, far above him, scolded the unwanted, restless human on the ground. He had upset their prerogative of heralding the dawn.

Within the hour Hansen was on the trail again, still plodding toward Olympus.

His only alternative was to return as fast as possible to the ranger station and have Pete Baker broadcast to the fire lookouts and other stations that Nadine had disappeared. But the terminus of the Hoh River trail was now the shorter distance by far, and Carl felt impelled to follow it to the end in search of her. When that was done, he might have no other choice than to retrace his steps along the river. But he could make that decision at trail's end—at the jump-off into the unmarked wilderness that lay between the glaciers and the Enchanted Valley.

It was the footprints that had crystallized his decision. He would go on beyond Elk Lake; and if there was no sign of Nadine, he would explore that dead-end side trail, as Fenner had done. The footprints were fresh; whoever or whatever had made them was in the area, and might go again to the foot of Ludden Peak.

In the dawning Carl saw that he was quite near the timber line now. There were no longer great giants in the forest around him. Now there was merely a scattering of sizable spruce and hemlock and cedar that had defied the mountain winds. The woodlands became gnarled and twisted here, struggling against the elements and the rocky, unfriendly earth. Still, the vegetation was enough to hide the Hoh from the trail. Hansen could hear the river now rather than see it. Here it was narrow and tumbling, a cold and lively glacier stream.

Almost with every yard, Mount Olympus loomed higher and more forbidding, its dark jagged spires seeming to rise in Hansen's path as he walked. It was an illusion that had turned back many a stranger to the trail and would turn back many more before the end of time.

But Hansen knew that the trail veered eastward, skirting Olympus and its dangerous glaciers. He knew that if he kept going, if he ignored the rumbling of his gut and the dryness of his mouth and the gradually growing ache of his bones, he should soon be reaching Elk Lake. And maybe by nightfall the end of the Hoh trail, and the weird foothills of Ludden Peak. . . .

The sun was well past its zenith when Carl caught his first glimpse of the lake. The sky was a pitiless steel blue. The tang of altitude, of ice and snow, was tempered by exertion and the bright sun. On the trail Carl was sweat-

ing. His woolen shirt was soaking it up and drying it into
his nose; his leather hatband was damply slick against his
forehead. Sweat trickled in his two-day growth of beard.

But his hunger had gone, miraculously, along with
ache and weariness. He knew he could keep on now in-
definitely. He could walk now in his sleep, until he had
found Nadine, or a sign of her, or given up to race for
the ranger station and spread the alarm.

It had occurred to him that he might find Fenner. Pete
Baker had said Fenner was out on the trails. But he had
not mentioned the Hoh trail specifically, and now Hansen cursed himself for not inquiring. The nearest trail
beyond the Hoh path was several days' travel through
terrain and vegetation far rougher than the Hoh basin.
The nearst fire tower was at least fifteen miles to the south
through unmarked country, Hansen recalled. The closest
ranger station in that direction was far beyond. At Ludden Peak it would be a toss-up whether to strike out for
the ranger station at Press Valley or the one at Graves
Creek, or return to Pete Baker's bailiwick on the lower
Hoh. The latter recourse would be easiest, quickest. But
there he'd be far removed from the search activities that
would be organized the moment word was broadcast that
Nadine Wade was missing.

Elk Lake widened before his gaze as he moved along
the trail. He resolved, at sight of it, to make Press Valley
station his next goal. There, by radiotelephone, he could
find out from Pete whether Nadine had passed his station
on her way to Illahute. If not, she could be anywhere at
all in the unknown areas between trails. As he thought
of this, Carl Hansen's dry lips closed in a grim line, and
his eyes squinted suddenly as if from physical pain.

Lifting his head skyward, he looked off to the west.
Heavy black clouds were moving in, spreading north and
south along the coast. As he watched, a serpent of yellow
lightning stabbed through the dark mass, and then another. He waited, straining his ears, but there was no
sound of thunder here. The rain, he knew then, would
not be tonight. At the earliest, if it came now at all, the
new precipitation would arrive tomorrow morning.

Eyes still on the sky, Hansen turned again toward the
lake. Suddenly his blood ran cold.

A movement, slight and curiously stealthy, had brought
his glance from the overhead blue that stained Olympus'

snow to the shade of polished steel. The movement was
in the upper branches of a spruce that was dying from
the top. The tree's roots had come to the end of their
usefulness against the outstretched granite feet of the
mountain. Its natural hydraulic apparatus could lift
nourishment no higher; growth had ceased long since.

Hansen's experience and instinct told him at once what
the lofty movement was, even before he saw the cougar
outlined against the sky. As quickly as it had come, his
fear subsided. The spruce was a fair distance from the
trail. Obviously Hansen was not the stalked prey. Whatever the cougar had marked for his own was on the lake
shore, probably a deer or an elk. As he watched, the movement in the heavier green ceased. He saw the animal itself moving out slowly on a barren branch. To Hansen,
the cat seemed skinny rather than lithe. Unquestionably
it had been wounded or ill, possibly unable to hunt until
now. That would explain not only its thinness, but also
its presence so near the timber line, perhaps its decision
to strike from aloft.

The relatively heavy rump was toward the trail. The
graceful tail waved stiff and slow, as if in rhythm to the
beast's intense scheming. Although the small head was
hunched down, almost hidden from Carl, he could imag-
ine the opaque amber eyes, cold and expressionless, fixed
on the defenseless prey below.

As a woodsman with respect for the natural laws of the
Peninsula, Carl was inclined to watch this silent drama
objectively. It was the law of the timber that the cougar,
too, must live if he could. It was known that if the yellow
cats were killed off in numbers too great, then eventually
the elk herds themselves overmultiplied. Their foraging
became too destructive, and finally they themselves suf-
fered.

Besides, Carl told himself, this scrawny cat deserved a
meal.

But somehow the thought of a gentler animal come for
the waters of the lake, or basking peacefully in the sun,
changed Carl's mind. He could doubtless scare the cougar
off, although its desperate condition made that a some-
what treacherous business.

There seemed to be no wind at all now, but Hansen
moistened a finger and held it aloft. Its cool side told him
the cougar was to the windward of him. Even as he tested

the wind, he was aware that Snoose had stiffened, stood stock-still in the trail, nostrils distended and forefeet wide apart. "Easy, boy," Hansen whispered, patting the animal's flank. "Easy, now. . . ."

Leaving the horse, Carl moved carefully into the brush, wanting to be sure what was on the shore of the lake. Deliberately he had left the .45 in the saddle pack. Snoose was already alarmed, and Hansen had no wish to attract the attention of a hungry puma to the trail horse. Besides, a revolver shot would be tricky, perhaps useless at that angle. But in his right first was clenched the handle of the runt machete.

Stalking toward the lake bank, Hansen kept one eye on the nearly motionless form against the sky. At any moment he expected the head to rise and turn in a yellow blur, fixing the amber eyes in a new direction. But now that tail had stopped; the hindquarters were more hunched. In his mind's eye Hansen could picture what could happen at any second—the cat body stretched and plummeting, legs stiff for the landing on the back of the prey, claws unsheathed. The glistening fangs would be ready in that brief flight, but there would be no sound throughout the flashing yellow arc. There would be no sound until the screaming of the unwary prey.

Then Carl Hansen's heart leaped into his throat like a hooked trout. Through the foliage he glimpsed the prey, dazzling white and gold in the bright sunlight, glistening from the waters of the mountain lake. Those opaque amber eyes, with death in their cold slant, were on Nadine!

In that instant of realization Carl thanked God for the fright that choked his voice. A human outcry would disturb Nadine as well as the mountain cat, and at this precise moment in eternity one movement of that white target could bring fang and claw from the quiet sky.

She had followed Carl's advice and taken her bath in Elk Lake. And now she lay drying in the sun as though asleep, one arm thrown across her eyes to shield them from that blinding blue sky. Her head rested on the crimson woodsman's shirt, her hair fanned out upon it in a cascade of gold and silver. The trail boots and the rest of her clothing were strewn across the shoulder pack fifty feet away. Carl saw that there was complete exhaustion in the gentle curves of her body, and realized she must have come up out of the lake only a few minutes before, to drop wearily where she lay. Now he knew that she must have begun her trek the very night the unspoken name of Murchison rose between them. If he had not stopped at the shelter he could have overtaken her.

Deliberately, almost gently, he swung the machete in a slow half circle through the brush. It could have been the noise of a clumsy bear, and the sharp ears of the cougar picked it up. The cat did more than raise its small head; it turned completely on the branch in a movement so quick that Carl could not see it happening. He knew only that now the yellow cat's gaze was on him, and that Nadine had not moved.

He went forward again, slowly. He had no idea what the cougar would do now, but clearly the animal was equally puzzled about the man. The yellow head lifted slightly, looked for an instant beyond Hansen and then to either side. Hansen stepped forward once more, noisily, brashly, waving the machete before him. Suddenly the big cat slid toward the main trunk of the spruce and climbed higher.

"Nadine!"

Hansen shouted it at the top of his lungs, his voice sharp in warning, commanding. He was ready to shout it again, but out of the corner of his vision he saw the swift movement, the red shirt flashing against the blue of the lake. He heard her startled, half-muffled cry.

The mountain cat was still on the move. Carl sensed that it was nervous now, more than ever puzzled. He kept moving toward the spruce, chopping at the brush with the machete. Then the yellow beast above him ran out on another branch, higher this time, gray and leafless. There was a sudden crack, like a pistol shot through the forest. Hansen saw the cat falling heavily, still clinging to the dead branch. He heard the thud that meant the cougar had struck the ground, and at that sound Carl ran fast and swung the machete in a hatchet movement with all his strength.

The animal was still half stunned as Carl ran in. Had the cat fallen free, or leaped, it would have been on its feet and springing. But the failure of the dead branch had surprised it; the claws had bitten deep into the gray wood, and the dirty yellow body had not twisted in time.

There was a roar when the machete cleaved the small

head almost to the killer's eyes. The cat jerked nearly upright, snarling and slashing, its blood spraying Hansen's
face. The machete swung again, this time like a broad-
sword at the thick neck. It was wrenched from Carl's grasp
by the final strength of one blood-smeared paw. But it
didn't matter now. The mountain cat teetered awkwardly
on its haunches, all its feline grace running out with its
blood, and the battle was done.

Hansen fell back against the spruce for a moment,
panting. His face felt sticky and he wiped it with the tail
of his shirt. Then he picked up the runt machete, wiped
it against the mossy ground, and drove the tip of its blade
into the spruce trunk. It would be useful again. But he
hoped not like this.

"Carl! Oh, my God in heaven, *Carl!*" He looked up.
Nadine stood now at the top of the lake bank, trembling.

At his shout she had leaped to her feet and swung into
the crimson shirt, hurrying toward the trail. There she
had seen the cougar for the first time as it fell with the
dead branch, as Hansen rushed into the clearing with
machete clenched above him. Now her shaking fingers
could make little use of the shirt buttons. Her red mouth,
after speaking in that breathless whisper, gaped loosely.

She tried again, swaying. "Carl, I . . ."

He ran at her, seemingly with the same fury with which
he had charged the mountain cat. Nadine had witnessed
that fury. Now his beard was dark, his face transformed
with splattered blood; and she remembered the strange
anger of two nights ago. She stepped back fearfully and
would have fallen if he had not caught her in his arms.

"You fool!" he said hoarsely. "You little fool!"

He kissed her, unmindful of his bruising beard. As he
lifted his face he saw that her own cheek was smeared
with the puma's blood. For a crazy moment it frightened
him, and then he laughed. "It's the lake again for you,"
he said, searching her eyes. "This time with a bodyguard."
Again he kissed her, long and hard. Her arms went round
his shoulders, not slowly, but so fiercely that they almost
lost their balance on the mossy bank of the mountain
lake. . . .

Far back in the woods, across the trail, a black she-bear
with cubs ambled awkwardly in the general direction of
the lake. She was making a wide detour because she had

smelled horse, which probably meant that man was around somewhere. The she-bear did not exactly fear man, but you could not always be sure about a horse if it became frightened enough to attack. And the cubs were along.

She crossed the trail well above Snoose and was plodding slowly toward the lake, the cubs tumbling beside her, when the fresh smell of the cougar carcass struck the blunt twitching nose. That was curious enough, but the sounds from the lake were not the wet plunging of the bull elk, or his stentorian call. These were human voices, certainly, and happy enough. The old she-bear knew the sound of the human voice in friendliness; in fear and pain, too. But somehow this was different. Never before had the black bear heard the laughter of two humans together in quite this way.

The inherent curiosity of the black she-bear pulled hard. The mingled smells of horse and fresh cougar blood, together with strange sounds from humans threshing and playing in the mountain lake like cubs—it was all a combination worth a bear's investigation.

But mother instinct proved stronger than curiosity. This was far too strange to risk. She and her cubs could drink from the Hoh, and leave the swimming lesson for another time. In a swift, surprising burst of speed she circled around the cubs, her low growl warning them. Then she nosed and pawed them head over heels in the opposite direction, back toward the trail and beyond to the rippling Hoh.

Overhead a buzzard wheeled in a great circle that traced the lake shore and encompassed the dying Sitka spruce. Already the dead top branches were black with crows.

Carl Hansen did not mention the strange footprints to Nadine, nor did he tell her why he wanted to take the dead-end trail to Ludden Peak. To explain this detour on the way to the Enchanted Valley he had to tell her a half-truth. "Pete said that Fenner, one of his rangers, was out inspecting trails, remember? We haven't run across him yet, and he might be out toward Ludden Peak."

Nadine smiled. "Lonesome?" she asked.

"You know better than that," Carl said, slipping an

arm around her shoulder. He grinned down at her. "But I thought Snoose might be, going back on the trail alone. Fenner could keep him company."

But Herb Fenner was nowhere on the Ludden trail, nor did Hansen see a sign of what he sought.

Relieving Snoose of his burden for the last time at the Hoh trail's end, Hansen scribbled a note and tied it securely to the horse's mane. It read simply: "Pete: Snoose has been a wonderful help. We thank both of you." Should he report the strange footprints in the meadow of the rain forest? He decided against it. There might be some perfectly plausible explanation. Pete Baker had been rather keyed up about the wild man, and a mention of those footprints might set off an alarm that could be embarrassing later. Carl signed Nadine's initials and his own to the note, added the date, and let Snoose go. The little animal jogged happily toward the home corral. There was no visible sign of regret, and Hansen laughed as the sleek hurrying rump disappeared beyond a stand of gnarled mountain junipers.

"We'll have to cache some stuff here," he said, squatting before the waning fire. "Can't carry the works from here to the Quinault." He grinned at her wryly. "And I brought Snoose along to help break you into the trail! I needn't have worried, looks like. Tell me. You took the pocket map with you—does that mean you'd have gone on from here alone?"

"If you hadn't found me, Carl, I wouldn't even have got to the end of the trail." She shuddered, gazing at the fire. "You haven't forgotten the cougar already?"

"No," he answered. "But I was thinking of something that could have been worse." He nodded eastward, toward the dim outlines of the peaks of the Olympic range —Graywolf, Deception, Jupiter, The Brothers. "You were going back in there, off the trails, when I had most of the gear and the rations."

She didn't reply, so he knew that he was right. Slowly he said, "The mountain cat would have been quicker, you know."

Her continued silence told him she understood this quite clearly. He thought: Of course. Johnny Wade did just that. So why not his daughter? That's how she might have been thinking.

Then she added something, as if she had been reading

his mind. "You can't tell. I might have got through, you know. I had the map."

He looked at her clear profile in the firelight, delicate yet somehow strong, too. Her chin was lifted a little; all the Wades and Baker-Smiths were proud and stubborn. "Yes," he said. "You might have made it. You have the map and you're not afraid. But you might *not* have made it—and you knew the chances of that, too."

Her smile was curiously indirect. "Fifty-fifty, would you say?"

He moved closer, taking her hands in his own. "That's the part that gets me. That's the part I don't like, Nadine."

There was a soft hissing from the fire. Tiny craters appeared in the gray ashes at the outer edge of the blaze. It had begun to rain softly, warningly. That heavy dark mass had moved in from the coast, its moisture holding. But by morning it would let go. As if the jagged granite peaks had punctured it, it would all let go.

"You were angry," she said quietly.

"I was a little crazy. I was a fool."

"Whatever you were," she went on softly, "you didn't seem to want me. I could have gone back to—to Illahute." Had she substituted the name of the town for Murchison's? "Or I could keep on going, as we planned." She was looking at him now, squarely. Even in that semidarkness her eyes were startlingly blue. "There wasn't any other choice, I thought."

The fire was choking now. It was slowly drowning from great intermittent drops that fell like pebbles from a cliff. Nadine's soft lips were half open, quiet. The pink tongue behind the white strong teeth made no sound. Yet her voice came softly, and from a great way off, drifting to him through the rain forests and through the years. It came to him through both time and distance, her voice, yet he could distinguish the words clearly: "You can keep the rain away from me, Carl."

"Nadine!"

That was his own voice. That much he knew. But he did not know whether he cried out her name here, in the wilderness, by this dying fire, or whether it had come with her own, through time and distance.

It did not matter.

Chapter Fifteen

By MORNING it was raining in earnest. The aspect of everything around and above and beneath them had changed overnight.

Yesterday the sky had been like fine stainless steel, polished and rolled, pitiless with glare. The mountain lakes and streams had been indigo, the tiny snow trickles as opaquely white as icicles. Now both water and sky were gray. Even the snows of the bigger peaks were gray now, seen through the gray fog, the gray mist, the rain that looked as if it might stain skin and clothing gray as it pelted down at angles dictated by the vagrant winds of the range.

But gray granite had become black, glistening; and the mossy patches of the timber line were now too dark for green and brown. The strongly ridged trunks of the taller conifers were soaked as if with ink; their needled branches were charcoal smudges against the sky.

Yet Hansen knew that the storm had only begun. He remembered those clouds that had been building up far beyond the coast, above the great Pacific. He had seen them rolling inland, spreading north and south as they came. He had glimpsed the yellow fire in them, imagined the crashing thunder. Now they had stretched over the center of the Peninsula, in the night, like a black tent. There they would hover, Carl knew, until empty of rain, of sleet, of misty fog, of jagged lightning.

But he and Nadine had slept well, lulled by the sounds they had known so often from their births in Illahute, soothed by the smells of rain on growing things. They had slept dry, snug in sleeping bags beneath the canopy of Douglas fir, with ponchos wrapped around the sleeping bags.

With some difficulty Carl built a small fire underneath the fir's protection, to make coffee and fry bacon. But when he said, "Looks like we're in for it," there was neither concern nor irritation in his voice. And Nadine said only: "It looks that way." There was no hesitancy, no talk of waiting out the rain beneath the cedar boughs. It is never wise to wait out rains in the Peninsula. They too can wait—and meanwhile the rations run low, the stamina fades, and the wet cold creeps easiest into legs that are motionless, into lungs not working deeply on the long trek.

They skirted the tips of the glacier called White, and the one called Blue—both dirty gray, now, in the steady downpour. They found Ice River, and tracked along it. They bisected Bear Pass and Marmot Pass, and began the slow descent from the timber line down again into the deeper rain forests between the Hoh and the Quinault.

The runt machete had plenty of work now. No rangers had cut the way here. But Hansen could raise the outlines of Olympus, behind them now, and Stone Mountain, beyond which the Hamma Hamma ran. For the time being, this was his compass, his line of direction. The machete swung almost ceaselessly, throwing rain spray from decapitated jungle growth; the machete moved almost with the rhythm of Carl's legs, and Nadine came close and steadily behind him.

Sometimes there was a word or two between them, but more often not. Words could wait until noonday or dusk, or until a midmorning fire built to dry pants and boots a little if the wind was running cold. Their flannel hats were shapeless now; the rain cascaded in rivulets down the folds of their ponchos.

The rain was more than ceaseless now; it increased in intensity, in density, in sheer cacophony against countless leaves and needles and tufts and rocks. It became the only sound, like all sounds together in the forest at night.

It became, at last, the silence of the dark Peninsula.

And finally it became also a curtain against the sky, and then against the tall peaks, one by one. Graywolf disappeared from Hansen's sight, then The Brothers and Jupiter. By late afternoon Deception had flickered off the horizon like a black beacon, a ray gone dead and useless.

When he could no longer see Mount Anderson, tallest of all except Olympus, Carl stopped. "We'll make camp here," he said. "It's nearly night, anyhow." But he had to look at his watch to be sure of that; the light had changed little since noon.

Turning to the north, behind them, Hansen saw that Olympus, too, had dropped off the horizon, like all the others. "Until morning," he grinned at Nadine, "we're as good as lost." He unslung his pack beneath a spread of hemlock boughs. "Let's have a look at the map."

Wet fingers slid into the pocket of the crimson shirt beneath the poncho. Her eyes fastened on his. "It's—I must have lost it there on the bank of Elk Lake!"

Hansen shrugged. "It doesn't matter. Tomorrow when we can see the peaks . . ."

But the peaks were not visible at dawn or at midmorning, when the pair moved on again. Even Olympus was still hidden. The rain kept coming down. There was the feeling now that it would never stop, that it must keep on pouring like this until the world's end. Hansen knew that feeling; so did Nadine Wade, and it brought no panic to them.

Yet the going was tougher now, much tougher. When there was not black mud, the moss patches were dangerously slick. And the rot of fallen logs and underbrush seemed in the downpour to progress before their eyes. Almost nothing that looked solid could be quite trusted. Once Carl crashed to his waist on a fallen spruce that looked as solid as a growing tree. Another time, for almost a quarter of a mile, they floundered in underbrush that reached halfway to their knees.

Carl slackened his pace. Gradually he recognized that his direction now was chosen more and more by instinct, less from memory. He had been here, he felt certain; but how could one be absolutely sure when no bearings could be taken on the range peaks?

Hansen had not scorned a compass in omitting one from his gear. He simply had not thought of a compass. They were for tenderfeet, and Boy Scouts learning their outdoors. A man who knew the peaks, and the course of any major stream he found, had no real need of a compass.

But the peaks were gone now. If only one, if only Olympus would thrust the crown of its tower against the lowering sky!

It was the slope of the ground beneath his feet that encouraged Hansen to keep moving now. They had risen to a ridge, a divide, and he tried to follow it. Somewhere on that ridge, if ever the rain stopped, there was a place where you could look down on one side and see the beginning of the Elwha, and on the other, make out the silver serpent that was the birth of Quinault's north fork. Those rivers ran in nearly opposite directions; the Quinault and its forks generally westward to the Pacific sea, the twisting Elwha northward to tumble at last into the Strait of Juan de Fuca.

Then Carl Hansen realized ruefully that this need not be the ridge he believed it was. He stopped suddenly on the ridge and peered into the mist below, feeling Nadine move close against him, touching his hand.

"What do you see?" she asked.

He laughed shortly. "Same as you. Gray soup." He looked at her wet face; raindrops coursed down her cheeks like tears, but her eyes were unafraid and laughing. "If a minute ago that fog had opened up and I'd seen a river down there, I'd have sworn it was the Elwha. Half a minute ago I wouldn't have been sure whether it was the Elwha or the fork of the Quinault—something we've got to know," he added, a slow grin spreading over his dripping face. "But right now, if I saw a stream down there, I'd be wondering if maybe it wasn't the Ducka-bush or the Queets!"

"You mean we're temporarily lost again?"

Hansen had to laugh at the way she said it; her voice was as unbelieving as it was untroubled. He slid an arm around her waist and kissed the wet lips. "Until I can get a sight on those damned mountains again, we are. At least I know this much: We're not going to hit the Press Valley trail. Now it's get through to the Graves Creek station or—"

A flash of lightning tore the dark heavens into two jagged pieces; the thunder crash was almost instantane-ous. Now we'll get the whole of it, the works, Hansen thought. He dropped his arm but kept hold of Nadine's hand. "That means this ridge is no place to be," he said quickly, and started down.

There was an acrid burning smell in the air. The gray mist became yellowish and the rain ceased eerily for a moment, then began again with new fury. They were ten minutes down the slope when another streak of light-ning seemed to strike above and behind them. In the in-stant of the white glare he saw Nadine's face turned up-ward toward the ridge. The vibration of the thunder sent a stream of gravel and talus stones sliding against their boots. She knew why he had wanted to get off the ridge.

He kept to the descent, as fast as the rough wet terrain would let them. But in a moment Carl stood stock-still, frozen in the downpour. Far ahead, over the treetops below them, new clouds were moving in with the speed of an express train. But they alone were not what had stopped Carl in his tracks. It was a sound, distant at first, but growing—a sound that was a weird banshee cry.

"That wind," Nadine breathed. "Listen to that wind!"

Hansen was listening indeed. This was more than a mountain squall, a willawaw. It must be, he thought, a dozen willawaws combined into hurricane force and speed. In the next second came the proof. Above the screaming of the wind was the snapping of a giant tree, then another, and yet a third. The sounds ran together in a triple explosion. The echo dwarfed the falling of the trees, so that the familiar long *whoo-oosh* and the earthshaking crash were scarcely audible.

Carl whirled, pushing Nadine back up toward the ridge. Another lightning flash lit the way, brought the knife edge of the ridge into sharp relief against the sky. "We'll be safer up there now than—" Carl yelled against the banshee scream, but the following thunder drowned his words completely.

The lightning had revealed two upthrusting chunks of granite, black with rain, near the top. There were perhaps three feet of clearance between the two rocks, and Hansen led the way toward them, almost scrambling on hands and knees.

Behind and below them now was the sound of hell on earth.

Plunging between the granite shafts, Carl pulled Nadine after him. He braced himself against rock, locking his long legs around the girl's middle in a scissor grip. The banshee wind was not yet strong here, but no human could foretell the path and strength of willawaw. Hansen had seen them change course half a dozen times within four hundred yards. And this was a willawaw of hurricane force.

There was another series of explosions below them, closer now, Hansen clamped his palms against his ears like a vise, yelling at Nadine, "Do this—tight, *tight!*" They sprawled between the granite grotesquely, locked together, drenched, staring into the blacker pitch below them.

The lightning jabbed again, crackling. It burned a great hole in the mist and for a brief moment that seemed like eternity they glimpsed a path being cut through the forest below—trees of all sizes and shapes falling before an unseen scythe.

In the darkness that followed, the whole ridge trembled while spruce and hemlock crashed earthward. Against his back Hansen felt the granite rock shudder as though alive. The banshee wail grew nearer, filtering through Carl's fingers and against his eardrums. But now it was overhead, screeching above them like a Gargantuan bird seeking prey on the far side of the ridge.

Suddenly Carl stood up. He lifted Nadine to her feet. "It's over for now, but it may shift back." They moved down the ridge slope again, faster this time, heedless of the rocks and twisted juniper, until they reached the forest floor.

They skirted the holocaust created by the willawaw. The rain still pelted down, but the awful banshee cry was fading in the distance, beyond the ridge. Still, Carl knew, the wind currents might play around the ridge height for hours, spending themselves, to die with a zephyr's whisper on a mountain meadow, or vanish skyward with a witch's scream.

For hours they kept on. Carl hunted now for the trickle of a stream to follow. He had lost track of time, could not tell whether it was midday or dusk. His watch had stopped up there on the ridge, its mainspring snapped with the pressures of the storm. Once Nadine staggered behind him, fell awkwardly against his shoulders. He whirled to catch her in his arms. "I'm sorry," he muttered huskily. "We can stop here."

The girl shook her head. "I—I stumbled. It's all right."

He knew that it wasn't. He went on at a slower pace, watching for a grove that would give a little more shelter. His breathing told him that they had been climbing slowly, and he veered his course.

Quite suddenly the ground sloped downward, almost precipitously. Carl was puzzled. They had long since left the ridge. He might expect gentle valleys here; he hoped to find one. But this steep descent . . .

The lightning finally showed him. They were dropping into a great gash in the earth. There was no other word for it. This ancient depression was not a basin or valley. It was a gash, a great long slash deep into the earth's flesh, and undoubtedly the weapon had been a meteor.

With that clarity peculiar to lightning's glare, the seconds of illumination showed Hansen the vegetation below. It was revealed as the struggling cover of an old burn—a searing fire that had blazed perhaps half a thousand years ago.

The gash was a quarter of a mile long, he guessed, and maybe half that in width. The rocky floor, with its still struggling growth, had looked to be maybe four or five hundred feet below where they stood.

Suddenly Hansen realized that he was waiting in the darkness.

In the next flash of lightning he knew why.

At the deeper end of the long gash stood a tree whose size he would never have guessed or believed had he not glimpsed the depth of the meteor's plunge. Only its topmost branches would be visible around the horizon. They jutted hardly more than fifty feet above the level of the normal forest floor. Unless he stood on the very edge of this decline, no man could have guessed from a distance the immensity of the coniferous giant.

Carl felt Nadine clutch his arm in the darkness, heard her unbelieving gasp. "The great cedar!"

Yes, it was that beyond question. "Hogan was right," Carl said slowly. "And so—so was my father."

The outlines of the tremendous cedar were still in his mind's eye, seared there by the lightning's blaze. This was indeed bigger than the biggest sequoia known. It was far larger than any spruce or Douglas fir or hemlock Carl had ever seen in the dark Peninsula. For a western red cedar its diameter and circumference were doubly huge.

Nadine was still clutching his arm. "Should we go down there, Carl?" It was almost a whisper, almost fearful. He remembered that she had never believed in the great cedar, because Johnny Wade had never believed in it.

There could be no cedar larger than a redwood, Johnny Wade would reason. Cedars were usually smaller than the native hemlock and spruce and fir. Yet there it was, down there in the darkness. With the morning light it would begin to grow again, imperceptibly, as it had for hundreds of years.

Hansen felt he knew why that could be. The reason lay in the buried meteor, that once molten mass whose atoms

had mixed with this earth, helping somehow to nourish
the cedar's roots beyond men's belief. Some of the great
tree's strength had fallen literally from another world,
years before the seedling cedar had taken root.

Hansen covered Nadine's hand on his arm. "We'll go
down," he said. "You're very tired. Under that tree will
be a good place."

She was already sleeping by the time he had got a fire
going. Utterly exhausted, she had dropped in her
drenched clothes. But the ground beneath the boughs
of the great cedar was miraculously dry. He let her sleep.
There was no chill wind here; the fire and her body's
warmth would dry her clothing gradually.

When he was sure of her comfort, he examined the
huge cedar. The spread of its boughs was in keeping
with its girth and height. The lower branches were
closely set on the trunk; they were thick with lush needles of green. The long protected ground underneath was
a thick cushion of needles that had fallen and matted
through centuries.

In the shadowy flickering light of the fire Hansen
found half a dozen traces of initials. The few who had
stumbled onto the meteor's ancient path and found the
great cedar had wanted to leave something of themselves
there. But the thick bark was gradually erasing these
slight human scars. The growth had elongated the let-
ters, lifted them far above Carl's eyes, as if they had been
carved by giants.

In a moment he found what he sought, and caught his
breath. They were two straggly H's side by side, elongated
and almost illegible now. H. H.—Holveg Hansen.

So Holveg Hansen had been here, in all reality! He
had seen the great cedar, just as he had told Illahute.
Carl smiled crookedly, remembering what most of the
town had said. "It's the sort of thing a man like him
would think he saw. So he went back inside and got the
call to God? More'n likely he wasn't ten yards from the
highway, sleeping it off!" Well, who could blame them?
He hadn't really thought that Hogan had seen the tree.
True, he had believed in the great cedar more than Nadine; yet his was only a half belief. He had sided with
the town, not with his father. From now on, he knew, he
would think of Holveg Hansen in a new way. Yes, the
things his mother had told him, protecting Holveg in the

suspicious eyes of the boy Carl, had been near truth after all.

It was below the level of his eyes, on the tree's far side, that he found the fresh scratch that looked very nearly like J. It seemed to have been put there with a very dull blade or a jagged piece of rock. The mark was shallow; it could not last more than a year or two. But it could have been scratched there only last week, or the day before yesterday.

J—for Johnny?

Somehow it was the single first initial that made Hansen feel suddenly queer. Because the Johnny Wade he had known would certainly have carved J. W., and firmly. But this was a single J, shaky, infantile, only half impressed into the bark. Johnny.

Wade had never seemed aware that everybody called him Johnny Wade, and nobody within Carl's memory had ever called him just Johnny. Yet sometime in the dim past he must have been only that to his parents, to the kids he knew in school. Was this J for *that* Johnny? In an odd way that Hansen could not explain, and which chilled him now, the weak mark on the cedar's trunk looked as if it might be.

Yet maybe those footprints back on the Hoh trail were making him see something in this scratch that wasn't there, that couldn't be. Perhaps it wasn't a J at all.

But Carl Hansen knew that it was indeed a J, and something now made him sure that it had been scratched on the cedar bark during the dying storm. The knowledge came to him as if out of the damp night—a second before he heard Nadine's scream.

At the sound he stumbled around the soaking circumference of the giant cedar into the moving shadows of the fire. Nadine was not where she had slept. She knelt on one knee by his open pack, its gear strewn out on the forest floor. In her hand was his .45, and his glance flew to where the uncertain muzzle pointed.

"Nadine! *No!*" He ran forward, arm outstretched. The gun exploded as her finger clutched in stubborn paralysis at the trigger, but now the weapon was in his hand. Hansen moved into the brush, crouching, circling around the blackness where he had seen human eyes reflecting the firelight.

There was nothing where the glittering eyes had been.

He shoved farther into the soaking tangle, then stopped, listening. He could hear nothing but the lessening rain. It would be futile to search now, and it might be dangerous to the girl.

Stepping back into the firelight, Hansen pushed the safety catch on the revolver and shoved it behind his belt. Nadine was still on her knees, staring through him, he thought, and into the darkness of the rain jungle.

"It was a man," she said dully. "I saw his face. A bearded man. He was watching me when I opened my eyes."

Carl took her in his arms. He hoped his quiet laugh was gentle enough, steady enough. "More likely a civet cat or a bear," he said. "I thought it . . . might be a ranger." He stopped, smoothing her hair away from her face, his mind racing with thoughts of what he might have to tell her. But not now. "Try to get to sleep again," he said.

She shook her head. "It was a man's face, Carl. I'm sure."

"There was nothing there. There'd be no reason for—for a man to run when he saw me make your shot go wild." But had it gone wild? Might not Johnny Wade be lying out there in the wet green darkness, dying after two years of using his wits and skills against everything the dark Peninsula threw against him? "It's sleep you need," he said. "Tomorrow you'll know that some of it was a dream."

Her eyes met his, seeming to say she knew he didn't believe that. But she said nothing more. Leaning back wearily against the great tree, she only half closed her eyes, squinting at the waning fire. Hansen watched her, wondering whether she was slowly and painfully connecting that bearded face, those wild glittering eyes, with her old belief that Wade could be alive. Hansen had seen nothing in those eyes that reminded him of Johnny Wade; yet he could not rid himself of the eerie feeling that in them had been their own kind of recognition, an almost pitiful eagerness.

Neither of them actually slept that night. But they must have sat in a trance of exhaustion toward dawn, for they did not remember when the rain stopped. Hansen looked out at the sky where the dawn was breaking, and breathed a sigh of relief. He had been traveling generally southward, and that was good. The early-morning sky gave promise of being overcast, but there were no clouds or mist. Today, he was sure, he could see the higher peaks and get his bearings.

While Nadine prepared coffee he tramped beyond the cedar's meadow, retracing his steps of last night. When he returned to the fire he hoped that he was concealing what yeasted in his troubled mind. Nadine's glance fastened on him, questioning. Trying to smile, as though still dismissing her fear as a dream, he shook his head. "Couldn't find a thing except something that could have been a bear track," he said.

Not a bear track, he kept thinking. Those formless tracks he'd seen midway on the Hoh trail. He squatted on his haunches, breathing deeply. "That coffee smells good," he said. "A mug or two of that and we should run into a fork of the Quinault by this afternoon. With luck, the Enchanted Valley by tomorrow."

She tried to smile, but plainly her thoughts were troubled too. "Not lost any more?"

Hansen laughed. "We never were lost." He had an uneasy feeling that it was more true even than he meant. For they had an odd protector, he knew now. Johnny Wade or not, the wild man of the Peninsula had been with them since he'd found those prints in the meadow near the Hoh. From somewhere in that tangle out beyond the big cedar, he must be watching—just as surely as he had watched Fenner that day at the foot of Ludden Peak.

Chapter Sixteen

As THEY MOVED UP out of the meteor's strange canyon, Hansen debated whether to tell Nadine of the scratched initial on the cedar, the footprints, and Fenner's story.

All his reason, all his feeling for her, set him against these revelations. There was still the chance that last night's appearance of the man would be the last. If the man was actually Wade, and as yet hadn't made himself known—for whatever reason—there was the chance she would leave the rain forest with her belief laid to rest.

But suppose he told her what he knew? If she connected the horror of those glittering eyes with her father, God alone knew what the reaction might be. Surely she would realize then, as Hansen was now convinced, that the man was mad. And with a madness far deeper than the disturbance that first had sent him into the center of the Peninsula.

Time and distance, Carl thought, would erase some of the nightmare that had attended their discovery of the great cedar. It had been time and distance through which the old Nadine had come to him. It had been time and distance through which they had come together again.

Yet now the shadow of a strange Johnny Wade lay over the Enchanted Valley when at last they saw it spreading before them. It had been a shadow that he was sure crept unseen along their way through Bear Pass and Marmot, that skirted the Elwha basin with them, and followed the twisting course of No Name Creek. It was a shadow that transferred itself to Hansen's thoughts and which, against his will and helplessly, he transferred to Nadine.

As they camped along No Name, she said musingly, "Over that next ridge is the valley we came to see, you said last night." She looked up at him. "I—I'm almost afraid to look."

The remark startled him. But she did not seem to be thinking of the eyes that watched her from beneath the great cedar. "Why?" he asked. "Because you think it may not be what you thought?"

She shook her head. "No. Once you said I couldn't

run away from Illahute—that there wouldn't be any escape, even in the Enchanted Valley."

"I know," Carl answered. "When we've seen the valley, we have to go back." His eyes narrowed grimly, and he added, "But now I'm looking forward to that. Aren't you?"

There was something in her eyes that was different from the old fear. "I was," she said slowly. "But now . . ." She hesitated. "I don't know how to explain it, but there's something . . ."

Yes. Something. He knew what it was, even if it wasn't yet clear to her. She had believed Johnny Wade might be alive. There is a difference between a belief and the dawning of a truth, a reality.

She tossed her head, laughing a little. "But we won't spoil the Enchanted Valley, Carl." The proud chin lifted, the eyes had their icy fire again.

He looked at her. "Nobody can spoil the Enchanted Valley," he said. "Nobody can spoil what's happened to us now."

Yet Carl Hansen wondered. He was not sure.

Next morning, topping the ridge beyond No Name, they saw the Valley through a pale green mist. Here was the veritable jewel box of the kingdom of Olympus.

For this valley was not large. Almost all of it was visible from where they saw it first, with the warming rays of sun climbing above Mount Anderson, touching a sylvan fairyland to life. Its sheer-walled canyons stretched for hardly more than two miles, but few had seen the like of such granite façades.

"Valley of a Thousand Waterfalls" had been scrawled on the earliest maps, but it had become, as if by common consent of those who had seen it, the Enchanted Valley. The rock walls swept down nearly three thousand feet, and at first glance all the thousand waterfalls seemed within their view.

As they topped the ridge and looked down, Carl heard Nadine gasp softly. Then they watched in silence for a long time, while the green light grew paler. The sounds that rose from the valley were like soft music: the faint, incessant bass rhythm of the countless falls, the steady rustling of the Quinault; the amazing fingers of the wind on the green harp strings of conifer, willow, alder, maple, cottonwood, and the soft cedar called Alaska. But always the motif of the symphony was timelessness; all the music, the wisdom, the poetry and beauty of all the ages men have lived were there between the canyon walls.

The proof of that were the fallen tree giants strewn over the valley floor, great sleeping spruce and Douglas fir, stretching horizontal two and three hundred feet under blankets of thick wet moss. Some of them had fallen there in the time of Columbus. They had been standing proudly when the slant-eyed ancestors of red Indians trekked east and south along the land bridge now called the Aleutians, now only islands.

Some men called such trees dead—decaying, rotting. But Carl Hansen knew this was not accurate. Growing from almost every one of the downed giants was a row of new trees, of all ages and sizes, roots deep in the old trunk. They stood in a proud straight line, like soldiers. The valley was filled with such regiments under which the old logs had disappeared into the black earth.

Nadine spoke at last, almost reverently. "You were right, Carl. No one can spoil this."

He smiled, neither agreeing nor contradicting. She had not seen the whirling dot in the sky that he recognized as a helicopter. It was a long way off, and descending, but its presence back inside the Peninsula troubled him. More than likely, he thought, it was a Forest Service plane, out to survey the damage of the storm. But it could mean other things: a search, an alarm, tragedy in the wilderness, or—or the capture of the wild man.

He turned away, watching Nadine's rapt profile. Following her gaze, he saw the shining ice caverns beneath snow patches that rarely left the upper reaches of the canyon walls, the infant glaciers that hung on the lower slopes. A small herd of elk moved like toy animals, their graceful necks bent to the lush forage of the valley floor.

At some wordless signal between them Carl and Nadine started the slow descent. Brown squirrels scolded gently, running ahead and watching with bright tiny eyes. Two winter wrens streaked from tree to tree above them, ushering them into the valley of enchantment.

They moved like awed and respectful pygmies along the floor of the valley, around the great trees, across the meadow patches bright with huckleberries and maidenhair and oxalis. Above them now the waterfalls were like the bridal veils of Amazons.

That night, by the fire, her head in Carl's lap, Nadine smiled up at him. There was no fear in the blue eyes now, no troubling memory of the great cedar and the storm. But there was a faint sadness in them. "I wish we could stay here," she said, "forever."

He had been thinking that, too. "Maybe . . ." he answered slowly. "Sometime."

But he felt they were watched from the darkness beyond the firelight. The memory of the helicopter made him wonder about Hogan and the show at Hemlock Creek. It reminded him of Murchison, too.

He averted his eyes from Nadine's. When a man had found a valley of enchantment, why could he never keep it for long? Why had the great cedar been more beautiful in half belief than in the reality?

Those were good questions, he knew. Damned good questions. Somehow he figured that a guy wasn't supposed to know the answers.

But he knew that tomorrow they must leave. Tomorrow they must hit the Quinault trail and check in at Graves Creek Station. By now Pete Baker would have passed the word there. He looked down at Nadine, saying nothing.

At noon of next day, much to Hansen's surprise, Pete Baker himself confronted them on the Quinault trail, four or five miles from the Graves Creek Station. He was mounted. Two saddled trail ponies were strung out behind him.

When Hansen saw the saddle horses he did not need to read Pete's face. The jollity was gone. Even the ranger's relief at sight of the pair was short-lived. He tried to smile down at Nadine; and Carl, sensing the news that was coming, wanted to head him off.

"What are you doing on the Quinault, Pete?"

"Looking for you two," the ranger said briefly. "Flew across in the helicopter and picked up these horses from Proctor at the Graves Creek Station." He looked at Nadine again, his eyes troubled. "Better climb aboard and let's get back to Graves Creek."

The ranger was trying to hide his urgency, but Hansen felt it. "Are you putting me under arrest, Pete?" he asked, grinning.

"I can't arrest you," Pete said soberly. "Not for this. But you might as well know that Hunsicker, the sheriff at Illahute, has a warrant for you. I got that on the radio three days ago."

"A warrant? What the hell for?"

The ranger looked more unhappy than ever. "Disappearance of Nadine, the radio said. I suppose it's abduction or something."

"Suspected murder, maybe," said Carl grimly. "Hunsicker would get out any kind of warrant Sarah Wade or Murchison told him to. Of course you had the report we passed through to the Hoh trail?"

Pete Baker shook his head. "It wasn't over the ranger radiotelephone. I don't hear everything that's on the commercial radio broadcasts. You and Nadine are checked out from Hoh in my regular report, but that's not mailed yet. Except for Proctor at Graves Creek, nobody knows you two are in here." He hesitated. Then: "That is—there's one other person now."

Hansen stepped closer to Nadine, slipped an arm around her shoulders. "You mean Hogan," he said. "Hogan and the crew at Hemlock Creek."

Pete Baker looked at him beseechingly. He slipped down from the saddle and stood in the trail. "I mean Johnny Wade," he said. "He walked into Graves Creek last night."

Carl felt Nadine go limp beneath his arm. Then she tightened and said slowly, "I think I was beginning to know it, Carl." She straightened, moving toward Pete Baker. "He's— Is he all right?"

The ranger's answer did not come quickly. "Physically he's O.K. I brought a doctor in the helicopter, after Proctor gave me the word on the radiophone last night." He stopped, searching for words, then went off on another tack. "I was checking in for you and Carl, like I promised to do."

"But . . ." She let the word fall between her and the ranger, questioning with her eyes.

"He's—he's lost track of some time," Pete faltered. "He saw you and Carl back there, watched you just like he watched Fenner that day. Says he lent Carl his car to drive you and some of your school friends to Port Angeles, and Carl never brought you back."

There was a tiny rasping sound within her throat and her eyes were wide with a nameles dread as she looked at Carl. "I must hurry," she said in a half whisper.

Pete Baker nodded softly, almost glad that his news was done. Hansen moved to help her into the saddle. "You're sure you can ride?" he asked.

Back came that curious half-smile which always twisted him inside. "I'm all right now," she said. The smile widened bravely. "You see, Carl? I *always* knew."

Pete swung onto his own horse. When Hansen was astride, Pete bridled alongside him. "That warrant," he said. "Things are shaping up funny in Illahute. I should have chased after you the day you and Nadine struck out. You hadn't been gone twenty minutes when I got word the Golden Slipper had burned down."

Hansen swung around in his saddle. "Angie! What about Angie Skykomish?"

"She's all right. Wasn't there when it happened. A woman set it off—Buck Flack's wife."

Hansen's mouth was a stark line, his eyes narrow slits. Buck Flack's wife—or Murchison, with an oil-soaked ball of rags. Involuntarily he struck his boot heels into the pony's flanks.

"I'll want you to fly me to Hemlock in that coffee grinder," he said. "I'd better drop off there, before I go back to Illahute."

Chapter Seventeen

THE HELICOPTER lifted easily from the corral meadow of the Graves Creek Station. In the tandem seat behind the pilot were Carl Hansen and Pete Baker.

Only Proctor had seen them off. For nearly an hour now the doctor had been on the telephone, connected with Tacoma, making arrangements with a specialist there. Since her arrival at Graves Creek, Nadine had never left the room that Proctor had given over to her father. Carl Hansen had not seen her from the moment the door closed on her and the physician. Carl accepted that, on the doctor's strong advice; but he hadn't liked it.

Yet the doctor impressed Hansen. He seemed to make sense. Most doctors would have had Johnny Wade in the helicopter by now, transporting him to some gleaming city hospital "for observation." That would be the worst thing in the world for Wade right now, this man said. Physically there was nothing wrong with Johnny Wade. After two years in the wilderness he was far more rugged than most men his age. There was not even a trace of malnutrition, the doctor said.

"So I'm getting Hoskins to come from Tacoma," he said. "My idea is that he should come here for a talk with Wade—maybe for a week or ten days. The patient has to return to so-called civilization with some—er—preparation. There are certain— Perhaps hallucinations is too strong a term. Delusions, I should say. That is to be expected."

Hansen had nodded when the doctor peered at him sharply. Pete had told Carl about the chief delusion. The sight of his daughter and Carl Hansen on the trail together had taken Johnny Wade far back, to that rainy Sunday afternoon when Carl had driven Nadine and her friends to Port Angeles in Johnny's fancy Packard.

"He found you back in the Peninsula," the doctor said. "He trailed you for days and nights. Then he came here to Graves Creek and reported the matter. His own daughter had shot at him, poisoned by you. So he demanded your arrest. Ranger Baker is taking you to the jail in Illahute." The doctor sighed audibly. "That, in essence, is how it seems to Wade now."

Hansen understood. And the irony was that Johnny

Wade could turn out to be correct. If Hunsicker served his warrant, Carl Hansen would find himself in the Illahute jail within twenty-four hours, and for substantially the accusation that was in Wade's mind.

"So for the present," the doctor had gone on, "the daughter must humor him. She must not leave his side for an instant. It would be unwise, I think, for her to reveal any—ah—loyalty to you. And most unwise for you to face Wade at the moment."

Carl had asked, "Is there a chance he'll come right side up after all this time?"

The doctor had shrugged. "That's for Hoskins, of course. My opinion is that it's quite possible. Perhaps within some limits. The fact that he has forgotten the period of trouble that drove him to seek escape—I have an idea that may be an advantage."

Now, aloft in the helicopter and speeding northward toward Hemlock Creek, Hansen smiled grimly at the recollection of that opinion. If Johnny Wade temporarily had no memory of Jake Murchison, then he had no memory of the power Murchison held over him. You can't blackmail and persecute a man who doesn't remember his guilt, who doesn't even know you, Murchison, he thought. So now things are between you and me.

"There's the mouth of Hemlock," said Pete Baker suddenly, close to Hansen's ear. He gripped the logger's knee and pointed. "Say! Looks like . . ."

Hansen peered down through the plastic cab of the helicopter. Scores of spruce and hemlock logs were floating free in the Pacific's ebb tide. Another hour and they'd be far offshore. By the end of the week some of them would be washed along the coast from Tillamook Light to Cape Flattery. In a year the rest would be salvaged by Chinese junks and Jap trawlers, half a world away.

"Looks like one of your rafts busted up," Pete yelled.

Eyes on the horizon, Hansen shook his head. The sky was clear. The big storm was three days past, and Hansen figured the raft would have been made up since the rain winds smashed the coast. Weather hadn't set that pay load free, and Hogan wasn't careless.

Hansen leaned forward and tapped the pilot on the shoulder. He made a slow stirring motion with his hand, pointing down. The coffee grinder slowed, began to lose altitude, hovered like a giant awkward gull over the mouth of Hemlock Creek.

There was no sign of activity at the coast camp, but they saw the Ford roustabout by the side of the road that led to the highway. One of the high-cab tractors was parked at an angle in the creek, its towing arch tipped crazily.

The flying machine needed to go no longer for Hansen to see all that he wanted to see. The hood was off the roustabout's engine; a heavy sledge was still imbedded in the smashed motor. The Diesel of the tractor had been given the same treatment. Signaling the pilot again, Hansen jerked his thumb angrily upward, pushed a rigid forefinger along the course of the shallow creek. He saw four battered cars, half hidden in the brush.

The helicopter climbed at an angle, began following the creek bed inland. They had flown perhaps a mile inside when Hansen growled in relief and clutched Pete's arm. "They haven't made the operations yet," he said. The ranger followed his gaze. Below them a ragged knot of men plodded shoulder to shoulder, splashing eastward up the creek. There was a strange menacing determination about their formation. This was not a group of loggers on their business. This was a mob. These, Hansen knew, were Flack's men . . . and Flack was Murchison's man.

The pilot's head turned. Hansen signaled to stay on course. When the helicopter's peculiar sounds reached the mob, the red and brown hard hats were transformed to lighter discs as the men turned faces skyward. The machine's shadow crossed them, and they moved on again, still heading for the Hansen and Hogan show.

Within a few minutes after leaving the Flack gang behind, the helicopter raised the logged-off clearing and the still bright shacks that served as bunkhouse and mess shed. Even in the present danger Hansen could admire Hogan's industry. The swath was more than twice as big as it had been when Carl had left with Nadine for the Hoh trail. Dozens of fresh stumps greeted Hansen's gaze and he noted with satisfaction that Hogan had followed instructions. He was getting into the waste and the medium stuff, letting the big trees wait for saw-timber use.

Hansen leaned toward Pete Baker, hand outstretched. "Here's where I get off, boy."

The ranger's expression was one of protest, but he saw that Hansen meant it. Reaching down between his feet, Pete brought up the coil of hemp line, tapped the pilot's shoulder gently with its loop. The pilot nodded that he understood. Slowly, carefully, the machine hovered over the logged-off clearing and began its vertical descent.

Hansen left the tandem seat, crouching. "Want some help from Illahute?" Pete Baker asked. The logger shook his head. "I don't think there is any help in Illahute, Pete. I guess from here on this is Hansen and Hogan business."

One boot firmly in the loop of the line, Hansen sat on the floor, his legs hanging out the open door of the 'copter cab. All work had stopped in the clearing below. They had gathered quickly into an almost perfect circle, gaping upward. He saw Hogan's grizzled features upturned, picked out the near-white apron of the cook, and then to his intense dismay glimpsed Angie Skykomish, looking frail and small beside a tall redheaded logger. This was no place for Angie now.

The whirligig pilot was expert, and the ranger had handled the looped line before now. It was almost as simple as going over the window ledge of a one-story building, Hansen thought. His boots touched the slash between two great stumps. He let go quickly and signaled for the machine to climb.

"I'll be a cock-burned monkey! What a way to come back to work!" Woodpecker Hogan was slapping him on the back and wringing his hand. "Have a look, son! We been doin' all right."

"That's plain," Hansen said, facing them all quickly. "But downcreek we're not doing so good. The raft's been broken up, and the other tractor's out of commission."

Hogan's curse interrupted him. "Traitors! We got some danged traitors—"

"No, Woody. Our boys were badly outnumbered. They had to run for town, if they're not lying in the brush. Two men on the tractor and the watchman for the raft, against fifteen or twenty. They're coming up the creek now."

Angie Skykomish left the redheaded logger and ran to Carl, clutching his arm. "I knew it would happen! It's Flack, Carl. Buck Flack."

"Murchison, too," Hansen said grimly. He raised his

eyes to the crew. "We're outnumbered two to one, and
you weren't hired for this kind of business. Any man that
wants to hit for the taller timber can collect his check
now. And when it's over he can come back to work, if
there's still an outfit, and no questions asked."

There was a concerted growl of protest. Hansen had
insulted them, and it was what he meant to do. Hogan
chimed in, belligerent: "They won't skitter, son. And
every damned one's in training. Our redhead choker setter has picked a brawl with every logger that told him
Angie ran the Golden Slipper. That included everybody
but me!"

Hansen grinned at the flame-topped Hank. "Congratu-
lations," he said quietly. "You watch out for Angie.
There's a carbine in camp. Get it, and stay with Angie
at the shacks. I don't think this mob is armed. Murchison wouldn't try that kind of trouble—yet. But let any
man have it that tries to set fire to the shacks or the
slash."

He swung toward Hogan. "That leaves nine of us.
Figure we can all pile onto that tractor?"

"Mighty tight squeeze, son."

"All the better. Unhitch the tow arch, Woody. Bolt the
bulldozer shovel on her nose, and let's go." Hansen's
gaze took in every one of the crew. "Flack and his boys
are coming upcreek. We'll meet 'em going down!"

Hogan was at the controls of the tractor, Carl Hansen
by his side. Three of the crew crowded into the cab with
the partners. A pair of loggers stood jouncing on the
tail coupling, clinging to the cab stanchions; two more
perched on the hood of the Diesel. They carried peaveys
and hastily improvised clubs of spruce or hemlock,
snags intact.

Enjoying himself hugely, Woodpecker Hogan gave her
the gun from the start. Not far from camp the Diesel
turned a bend in the creek and met Flack's gang head on.
They had long since heard the roar of the tractor and
were waiting in its path, expecting it to be manned by
the usual crew of two with a tow of logs astern.

At Hansen's signal Woody brought the machine to a
halt a hundred feet or so from the mob. Hansen swung
out on the top tread, his eyes on Buck Flack. "This is as
far as you go, Flack."

At sight of Hansen the big unshaven logger showed

surprise. Then a cunning sneer spread over his face. "I don't think so, Hansen. There's a bounty on you. Reckon we'll take you back to town and collect from the Sheriff!"

The mob behind him cackled approval, brandishing peaveys, baseball bats, short-handled sledge hammers. One of the crowd waved a hand ax. Hansen noted the armament with more relief than concern. Murchison knew better than to send Flack and his cronies out with firearms—but nobody could guarantee that Murchison's orders would be obeyed.

"I said it was as far as you go." Hansen's eyes were still on Flack. "There's a choker setter back there with a thirty-thirty, Buck. Angie Skykomish is with him. He's going to marry her, and he don't like you at all, Flack. I wouldn't go."

Flack stepped out of the crowd. "You're through and don't know it, Hansen. The other tractor's busted and the roustabout is shot to hell. Your last logs are out in the ocean, Hansen, because I got an idea you might have a bad fire back in camp."

Flack liked the way his voice sounded. It sounded good to him against the trees. He no longer heard the throaty rumble of the tractor's Diesel as Hogan raced it a little. "The squaw chippy's lost her rooming house, and Hunsicker's got the jail ready for you. Somethin' tells me the pulp mill in Tacoma will figure you're just unlucky, Hansen."

He turned to the men behind with a wide forward motion of his arm. "Come on, boys. Knock 'em outa that buggy!"

Hansen stepped back in the cab. His voice was softly matter of fact. "We'd better get at it, Hogan."

It was fortunate the men on the hood and tail coupling were tense and braced. The tractor lurched ahead with an iron roar that echoed through the woods. The bulldozer shovel had been raised high. Now Hogan spun the wheel that brought it significantly down. For a moment, unbelieving, the mob stood firm—then realized almost too late that Hogan's whole weight was on the power rod and he wasn't stepping off.

The churning treads and menacing shovel literally split the gang down the middle. They scrambled for the creek banks, cursing. Croaking in glee, Hogan throttled the machine down, waiting for them to reassemble, decoying them into chase. When they were once more a crowded target, he spun the big woods equipment and repeated the performance.

That couldn't last. Following Flack's lead, they attacked with rocks from the creek bed. But that was not too effective; they knew they had to board the tractor. Hogan knew it too, and made it a rough business. If one of Flack's men tried it over the side, Hogan spun the iron monster around with the outside tread. When an attempt was made at the tail, the attackers met swinging peavey hooks, or Hogan circled the bulldozer shovel their way.

At one point Hogan caught a trio of Flack's gang before the bulldozer shovel and ran them up over the creek bank fifty yards into the timber, uprooting saplings and small trees in his attack, making even their escape a dangerous hell. When they crept back to the creek bed they found Flack staring in wary hatred, feet wide apart, his mouth open. He no longer had a mob. It was only a dispersed band beginning to feel helplessly ludicrous. The Indian yells of Hogan, the set grins of Hansen and the others on the tractor had made them doubt Flack.

"To hell with this, Buck," one of them yelled out. "It's like fightin' a goddamn Army tank!"

Hansen looked toward Flack. The man's eyes were wishing for a gun. They were telling Carl Hansen that one day he would have a gun, too.

Hansen gave Hogan a signal. The big Diesel quieted a little. "Your man's right, Flack. We can play this all day with you. Or you can head for the camp and let Hank drill you." Hansen paused, letting it sink in. "The fact is, Flack, you got just one minute to light out for the creek mouth. One minute—or Hogan drives down there and makes a scrap heap out of four cars parked in the brush."

There were angry howls of protest from the creek bottom. Flack's jaw hung slack. Bewilderment was behind the hatred in those little black eyes now. Hansen saw it, and pounced. Nudging Hogan, he broke into a loud, roaring laugh of derision.

Hogan joined it with his high frog croak, then the other men on the tractor. Hogan raced the Diesel, cracking the exhaust, letting the iron monster join the laughter.

Flack's followers looked at their leader, waiting. Four

of them wanted to keep their cars. The rest didn't relish the long trail to Illahute on foot. Slow contempt for Flack was rising in all of them, and he could feel it.

"We'll be back, Hansen. Depa-tized by the Sheriff. Armed, too."

Hansen's laughter broke into a slow grim smile that knifed even deeper at Flack.

"You couldn't raise a posse, Flack. Not after this. But you can tell the Sheriff I'll be in Illahute by morning— and you can tell Murchison, too."

Chapter Eighteen

RAIN FELL SOFTLY as Carl Hansen walked into the lower end of Illahute's main street early next day. The asphalt glistened black in the lowering mist. There was a gaping hole in the town's squat skyline where the Golden Slipper had been. The ashes were sodden, and the smell of drowned flame, of charred wood and mattresses and upholstered furniture was unpleasant in Hansen's nose.

Good riddance, some of the town would be saying. But there would be secret regrets, too, for laughter and song and quick, meaningless passions; for girls whose names would be remembered long after their bright faces had grown dim in memories.

Hansen crossed the street, choosing the board walk nearest the sea. He had spent the predawn hour on the winding trail from the Hemlock's mouth, watching the gray-white combers as he walked. Through the wet tule grass beside the path he had seen the little tug bearing down from Flattery through the rolling fog. The skipper would find no log raft waiting this morning. Hansen had left orders with Hogan to have the captain drop the hook and wait, weather permitting. It would be a long delay, Carl knew, with only one tractor in commission. He'd have to telephone Hollister and explain. That wouldn't be easy. Rumors floated by Murchison would have preceded Hansen's explanation. News had preceded him, too, by now—the "disappearance" of Nadine Wade; Carl Hansen's impending arrest; maybe the return of Johnny Wade to his log and lumber kingdom.

Hogan had sensed this had to be the showdown, and Hansen had had the devil's own time persuading the old codger to stay behind. Woody had brought Carl to the creek mouth with a tow of logs, and was for taking the trail to town with him. "You're headin' right into the band saw, flat on your back with your feet tied," Hogan said. "It's what I been scared of right along if you went back inside with that girl. She brought us trouble, got you loco for fair, and decoyed Johnny Wade back to life. None o' that is what a man could call sweet music, son."

"We'll see," Hansen told him. "Anyhow, it's more important you stay here."

144

And Carl stood on the trail for a time, listening to the fading throb of the Diesel on its way back to camp, half expecting to see Hogan sneak out of the brush, ready to shadow him.

Lifting his mackinaw collar higher against the rain, Hansen headed instinctively toward the old hotel. Funny, Carl thought; all this had begun there, and now it had to end there.

As he walked up to the gray wooden pile he saw the Sheriff rocking on the old front porch, squinting through the morning rain.

Hunsicker had been sheriff in Illahute since Carl was a punk kid, since the time sheriff was a full-time job rating a full-time deputy. But Illahute had grown steadily tamer. Hunsicker got only six hundred dollars a year now for being sheriff, and hauled feed and wood on the side. He didn't like the setup; it made him hate both those who insisted on arrests and those he had to arrest.

As Hansen came up the wooden steps, Hunsicker didn't get out of the chair or stop rocking. But he reached for his inner coat pocket, brought out a folded, crumpled paper. "Got something for you, Carl. Figured you'd come here, now the Golden Slipper's burned down."

Hansen took the paper. Without looking, he tore it into halves, dropped them over the railing of the porch into the rain. Hunsicker didn't even blink. "That ain't a good idea, Carl."

"You haven't got the word, Sheriff," Hansen said. "Johnny Wade is back."

The other nodded, still rocking. "I heard it."

"*He'll* be telling you again who's to go in the poky. Not Murchison."

There was a stir in the doorway of the hotel. "What makes you think Wade doesn't want you there?"

Hansen was almost afraid to turn and look at Murchison. Afraid of what he might do when he saw that beefy face again, that bright sport shirt open at the throat and the black hairs curling upward. It wouldn't do to lose control right now. Hunsicker sat there a witness, and always carried a gun.

But Hansen never turned toward the dark cave of the hotel's lobby. He heard the shuffling behind him, swung around toward the steps. But it was too late, and Buck Flack stood too close. There were the stained teeth behind

the sneering smile. There was the voice filled with hatred:
"I'm depa-tized now!" as the sap crashed against the side
of Hansen's skull.

Flack spat a nicotined stream between the bars, near
Hansen's feet. "So I'm to stick right with you, Hansen, on
account of the danger, see?"

Hansen sat on the edge of the dirty jail bunk, his head
between his hands. He was dimly aware that Flack, squatting astride a stool on the other side of the bars, had been
talking incessantly. Hansen's forehead throbbed and he
felt sick at the stomach. Only now was he able to make
out what Flack was saying. He looked up. "What danger?"
he asked dully.

"Why, the mob," Flack said, turning to him with the
sneering smile. "Ain't you been listenin', or have you
been dreamin' about how much fun you and Hogan had
yesterday with that tractor? There's been a threat to take
you outa here, Hansen, and the Sheriff don't like that.
Nobody's been taken outa here since he's been sheriff, he
says. So, I'm kind of protectin' you, see?" Flack laughed
thickly. "You know what they threaten, Hansen?"

Carl didn't answer. He looked briefly at Flack, then
away at the obscenities scrawled on the wooden walls of
the cell. Illahute's jail was only wood, but it was built in
the fashion of the old blockhouses of the Indian wars.
In one corner of the single large cell Hansen saw where
the wood had been deeply charred. Carl remembered how
a prisoner had tried to burn his way out, and been smothered in the smoke.

"People around here are pretty sore at you, Hansen.
Maybe you don't know it, but they are. Comin' back here
and givin' Woodpecker Hogan and Angie Skykomish big
ideas. Kidnapin' women. Bringin' in this pulpwood loggin'—as if things wasn't bad enough already with the big
outfit. I tried to warn you once, Hansen, but you were
too goddamn smart."

Hansen forced a grin. It made his head ache. "I know
it, Flack. You've been a good friend."

The burly logger snarled. "Still smart, ain't you? Well,
don't you want to know what they figure to do to you?"

"Let it come as a surprise, Flack."

Flack's mouth was already open to answer his own
question. But now he closed it momentarily, nodding his

head with badly suppressed eagerness. "O.K., I will." He added hastily, "Of course, the Sheriff and me ain't goin' to let it happen." Flack nodded toward the door that separated the cell and its hallway from Hunsicker's dusty office. "Tonight he'll be on duty, too." The stained teeth showed themselves again. "In here you'll be safe, all right."

"That's good," Carl said, lying back on the bunk. "Now knock it off, will you?"

His head kept on throbbing. He had no doubt that Flack had swung the sap again a time or two, while he lay sprawled on the hotel porch. Or maybe it was Murchison's foot.

He had no reason to doubt, either, that Flack was telling the truth about the mob. It wouldn't be too difficult to raise that kind of excitement in Illahute, the way things stood. If nothing else, Murchison and Flack could call on the gang that had been at the creek yesterday. They'd welcome a chance to get back at him and Hogan, particularly if it could be done without too much effort, in secrecy, and with the cloud of the warrant hanging over Hansen.

He realized now he should have got Hunsicker away from the hotel and got it through the Sheriff's head what Johnny Wade's return could mean. But Hunsicker always had been slow, and he'd figure to play it safe until Johnny actually returned to Illahute and made his condition known. Maybe he was right about that, too. Maybe that doctor had been too optimistic.

One thing sure: Jake Murchison didn't intend to wait around to find out. He was set now to take care of Carl Hansen first, and handle Johnny Wade again when the time came.

Hansen was awakened by a queer noise that sounded like a body hitting the floor. When he opened his eyes the little window near the ceiling was black with night. But there was a rectangle of yellow light splashed against the floor of the cell, striped with the shadows of the iron bars.

He rolled off the bunk and stood up. Through the open door leading to the office he saw Hunsicker stretched on the floor. His hat had rolled off; he was facing away from the cell, and Hansen saw the fiery red welt on his bald head. Two men were kneeling on the floor, hurriedly tying the Sheriff's feet and wrists together. One of those two men was Flack; the other was Murchison. Carl Hansen swore under his breath. So this was the mob!

They were going to make it seem the work of a mob. Done with Hunsicker, they went to work. Lifting the ancient swivel chair, Murchison splintered the panels of the outside door, then flung the chair into a corner. Flack overturned a wooden file case, grabbed one of its drawers, and crashed it into the room's single windowpane. Within three or four minutes the Sheriff's office looked as if a mob had passed through there on the way to the barred cell.

Hansen felt his hackles rising. Murchison had walked into the shadows and stood outside the cell door. Flack was standing behind his shoulder, waiting. Carl saw that he carried a coil of hemp. It had a hangman's knot, trailing the floor.

"Go in and shut the door, Flack. I want the handcuffs on him, and that rope around his neck—*tight*. I'll hold the gun on him. Go ahead."

Flack came slowly. He unlocked the cell door. "The key," Murchison said then, holding out his hand. When Flack was inside the cell, Murchison slammed the door shut quickly and turned the lock. Flack whirled around at the sound.

"Make it quick," Murchison said. "I'll open up when you've finished."

Hansen laughed with contempt. "He's careful, Flack. He's always been careful. He works on women—Sarah Wade, Nadine, Angie Skykomish. And old men like Henry Baker-Smith and Johnny Wade."

"Shut up," Murchison said, his voice shaking, "or we'll finish you off here." The muzzle of a .45 appeared between the bars, trembling a little.

Flack snapped the Sheriff's handcuffs over Hansen's wrists. Roughly the burning hemp scraped down his face. He bit off a curse as Flack jerked the noose closed. "Women and old men, Flack," he choked out stubbornly. "Those are Jake's specialties, Flack. He lets you handle the men." Hansen turned his contempt full on Murchison. "He used his sister to get started in Illahute. Did you know that, Flack? Used her alive, then her memory when she was dead."

Even in the shadows Murchison's features showed livid.
"Bring him out now." He turned the key in the cell lock
and stepped back. "Move, Hansen."

Hansen moved—but at the office door he pulled up
short, his voice rasping out, "Hogan! Get outside!"

Woodpecker Hogan had loped in from the rain, feeling
safe enough walking into the Sheriff's office, holding the
rusty carbine by its middle, like an Indian on the trail.
Murchison's .45 drowned out the sound of the cocking
lever as the carbine came up. Hogan's left leg flew back
from under him as if on a hinge; he was snapped flat on
his face. He rolled over, bleeding at the nose from the
floor's blow. He half sat up, trying to hug the shattered
knee. Hogan looked up at Murchison, his grin sick but
defiant. "I always wanted a wooden leg, you bastard!"
Then he fainted.

"Do it again. It's just his knee," Flack said.

Murchison shook his head. "Let him be. Nobody believes Hogan."

The hemp pulled tighter and Hansen felt a ring of fire
around his neck. Murchison's knee came up hard against
his rump. The three went outside into the wet rainy mid-
night.

They circled the jail and went down to the beach,
which was black with rain. The breakers were rolling in,
big ones. The trio walked the length of the town, past
the rear of the old hotel, and kept going. More than
Flack's gun was holding Hansen in; Murchison had the
other end of the rope looped around his middle. "Remember that big rock, Hansen?"

Carl didn't have to look where Murchison pointed. He
was already looking. There was where Holveg Hansen's
shack was perched when the big storm and the gray Pacific came for it.

"Too bad you weren't home that night," Murchison
said, as if he knew Hansen's thought. "But you're home
now. And now the breakers wash over it *all* the time
when the tide and wind are right. They're going to be
right tonight, Hansen."

Carl got it even before they marched him onto the flat
rock. Even before Flack began looping the other end of
the hemp around the base of the rock. "Quite a surprise,
all right, Flack," Carl said. "Glad you didn't give it away."

In an hour or two the Pacific would hang him. If the

first big breaker didn't throw him out to sea and break
his neck at the end of the hemp, an incoming comber
would smash him back at the rock for another try.

"Now his legs," Murchison said. "Make sure he can't
kick. And loop the end to the cuffs so he can't get at the
noose."

But I could drag you in with me now, Hansen thought
suddenly. I won't come out, but neither will you. Flack
was stooping at his feet, trying to straighten a short piece
of wet line. Hansen tensed in the darkness—just as a blur
of white moved down from the highway behind Murchison and Flack. A man in a white shirt. What man would
be as crazy as Woodpecker Hogan tonight?

Not a man.

Hansen wanted to yell, but now the rope was too tight.
He wanted to yell to high heaven like a beast of the timber, if they both died for it, he and Nadine together.

He'd never heard this voice. It was cold, almost cruel.
"Drop the gun, Jake. Stand up, Buck Flack. Drop that
rope and get away from there."

Murchison didn't let go of the revolver. But he didn't
turn, either; he didn't move even the edges of the bulky
shadow he made against the sea. Hansen saw the gleam of
a carbine lever. She must have Hogan's rusty 30-30; she
must have been to the jail. Hansen dared move his cuffed
hands to his throat now; he loosened the hemp. "Better
drop it, Murchison. Out there in the Peninsula I taught
her how to hate you."

The .45 clattered on the wet rock as Murchison whispered, "Rush her, Flack!"

Flack tried to obey the master's voice. The carbine
crashed and he screamed above the sea's roar. He
sprawled, jerking off the rock into the black wet sand,
clutching at his legs.

"That's from Hogan," Hansen said, watching Murchison in the blackness. "She's got another from Angie Skykomish. It hits a little higher."

"Stop it, you fool!"

The carbine's cocking lever answered Murchison. But
she spoke to Flack. "You're the fool, Buck Flack. There's
going to be plenty of work for all of you in Illahute now,
Buck. The outfit is going to log and cut lumber and pulpwood, and we're going to do it the way Carl Hansen

thinks it ought to be done. I've got my father's word for that. And now you've got it."

There was nothing then but the sound of the breakers, the wind in the trees beyond the road, the rain pelting down. Hansen thought he heard his heart, too, hammering. He knew Nadine was waiting for something. She couldn't see the handcuffs in the dark.

"Nadine?" Murchison's voice croaked it. "You going to shoot me in cold blood?"

"No, Jake. Kick that gun off the rock."

Murchison's foot moved. The .45 slithered into the sea. There was a swift overhead movement of Nadine's arm, and the carbine sailed heavily, end over end, following the .45. Flack cried out, "Don't! My God, he's got the Sheriff's cuffs on yet!"

Murchison rushed. It was quicker, heavier than Hansen expected. He staggered back with Murchison's fist against his mouth. He slipped on the wet granite and Murchison kept plunging. They fell flat on the rock, Hansen grunting with the impact of Murchison's heavy body. He couldn't get his linked wrists up, and the rope was still choking at his neck. Murchison was pounding his head with one fist, groping with the other for the rope's end.

Hansen drew up his knees, shot them forward with all the strength he had, and rolled. He got new footing, tried to loosen that burning hemp, but Murchison came again, crouching. Out of the blackness of the night and the years Hansen remembered something that had come down from the French-Canadian woods. He sprang feet foremost at Murchison. He caught the jaw, but his left boot fell short of the crotch.

Yet it had surprised Murchison, and Hansen propelled himself once more, kicking at the stomach this time. Hansen's arms were still locked at the wrists, and when he fell he got his own punishment on the salt-wet granite. It was a dangerous tactic for him, too, and his boots were not calked.

Murchison rushed again and Hansen swung the steel cuffs from his shoulder, like a ball bat, square against the beefy face. Then suddenly Murchison stooped, retrieved the trailing rope, and jerked hard. He had surprising strength on that hemp, killing strength. Hansen felt his tongue swelling even as he gripped the line with handcuffed hands, trying to break the pull.

"My dancing bear!" Jake Murchison whispered, glaring in the misty blackness out of wild, rolling eyes.

This man is mad, Carl thought suddenly. Madder than Johnny Wade ever was. Mad with hatred and fear. He knows I want to kill him. He's never been close to that before. "Dance, bear!" The hemp jerked again, burning through his clutching fingers. Murchison was drawing it in. "Keep hold of the rope," Murchison said. "You got to do that or choke. So now I'll do the kicking, dancing bear."

Hansen let him come now. A bear who doesn't want to dance can either fight the rope or embrace the master. Hansen encircled Murchison in the arc of his linked arms. Whatever strength was left must be all here and now, he thought, squeezing. It wasn't true that bears could kill like this, but Carl had seen the father of Angie Skykomish kill two this way.

"H-Hansen!"

It was hardly more than a whisper, but it was all Carl wanted. He kept on. A minute dragged by . . . two. Hansen's shoulders were knotted with pain, his arms were afire from socket to wrist.

Murchison's feet tried to shift, but Hansen was anchored now. Another minute, and Hansen moved his locked arms down just a little, toward the small of Murchison's back. He breathed deep and held that breath, hard chest against Murchison's softer one, rib and muscle against rib and fat. •

There was a faint rattling deep in Murchison's throat. His feet dragged now on the slippery rock like a doll's feet. Slowly, painfully, Hansen loosed the overstrained muscles of his shoulders and arms, the tendons of his forearms; his wrists were swelling inside the circles of steel. Murchison's bulk sagged into a shapeless sack on the granite that had been the foundation of Holveg Hansen's house in Illahute.

Carl turned at a new sound behind him. Buck Flack had dragged himself onto the rock, the Sheriff's keys in his fingers. Hansen thrust down his wrists while Flack unloosed him. "I'll send someone back to look at that leg, Flack."

Wordless, Flack moved to the shadowy form at the

rock's edge. With his uninjured leg he pushed Murchison slowly off, away from sight, into the gray combers. . . .

Now Carl Hansen swung toward the beach for a new embrace—an embrace that held neither hatred nor death, and no evil for him now. He felt the warm wet lips and there was a long time when he remembered nothing of the past or present, or what his future might hold in the dark Peninsula.

"Hogan," he said at last. "We must get back to Hogan."

"Pete Baker is with him," Nadine said.

"Pete?"

She nodded. "I made him fly me into town when he told me there was a warrant out—and what you found at Hemlock Creek. We went straight to the jail and there was Woody. And the Sheriff, who thought a mob had come for you."

"Johnny Wade?" Hansen said slowly.

"He's—he'll be all right, Carl. And what I told Buck Flack is true." She smiled up at him. "There'll have to be a merger, Carl. We'll call the outfit Hansen, Hogan and Wade from now on."

Carl grinned. "Hogan's O.K., but I don't want him between us. Make it Hansen, Wade and Hogan!"

He slipped an arm around her waist. They climbed toward the road, then walked toward Illahute, where they both belonged, through rain that seemed to Carl Hansen no more than a soft warm mist of promise.

THE END

of a novel by

Nard Jones